APACHE GOLD

Summoned by his dying father, Lee Keene
made his way to El Paso. Lee knew the old
man wanted to tell him the location of the
gold that he had been trying to find for
years. But the trouble was that Johnny
Hughes was waiting for him. Johnny hated
Lee and meant to kill him as soon as
he'd revealed the secret. That was bad
enough, but Manuel Ortega's banditos and
bloodthirsty Apaches also barred the way
to the hidden treasure.

APACHE GOLD

APACHE GOLD

by
Stack Sutton

Dales Large Print Books
Long Preston, North Yorkshire,
England.

British Library Cataloguing in Publication Data.

Sutton, Stack
    Apache gold.

A catalogue record for this book is
available from the British Library

ISBN 1-85389-705-1 pbk

First published in Great Britain by Robert Hale Ltd., 1995

Dales Large Print is an imprint of
Library Magna Books Ltd.
Printed and bound in Great Britain by
T.J. International Ltd., Cornwall, PL28 8RW.

1

As Lee Keene dropped from the stage-coach, the three o'clock west-Texas sun hit him full in the face. He stepped aside so that the other passengers could alight and, glancing up, took the black, leather valise the shotgun guard handed him before edging into the shade of the stage office veranda.

His intelligent gaze considered the dusty street, the brown hills forming a backdrop to the north and west. He had never seen such desolate country, and found himself again longing for the rolling hills, the tall grass, the thick pine forests of his native South Carolina. This land was a barren waste, and the hot oppressive wind flung grains of sand against his deeply tanned cheeks. He shook his head, wondering how anyone who'd known the south Carolina lakes and woodlands would tolerate this desert.

Footsteps scuffed over the hard-packed dirt. A man laughed inside the adobe coach office as the pungent odor of cigar smoke seared the air. Horses were tied to hitching posts along El Paso's one street while a few wagons collected near places like Juan's Tienda and Paco's Botega. A Saturday afternoon crowd moved in and out of buildings as harsh American voices mingled with soft Spanish accents. Lee stopped short as a well-known figure moved into view.

'I didn't expect to see you, Johnny.'

'I'm surprised to see you.'

'It's been about five years.'

'At least that. How about a beer?'

'I guess not. I have to locate George.'

'He's in the hotel. After your talk, come over to the cantina and I'll buy you that beer. It's good to see someone from back home.'

'I'll do that.'

When Johnny turned back into the cantina, Lee shouldered past its adobe front. The last time they'd met, Johnny had sworn to kill him, but time changed a man.

Reaching the hotel, Lee swung inside its cool interior. He approached the desk, signed the register, and took his key from a skinny clerk. 'I'm looking for George Keene.'

The clerk glanced at the register, then at Lee, nodded. 'He's down the hall, last door to the right. Your room's upstairs on the left.'

Lee climbed the stairs and tramped down the hall to number ten. The room overlooked the street, and hot air swept through the open window. Lee took off his coat and hat, studied the bullet holes in the walls, and shook his head. He tossed the bowler into a chair, removed his shirt, and walked to the washstand where he poured water into the large tin bowl. The water was stale and tepid, but the sponge bath refreshed him. The trip had been long, hot and tiring.

He pulled a clean shirt from the valise, shrugged into it, tucked the tail into his trousers, then stood before the window overlooking the street. A platoon of soldiers trotted by in a column of twos. A grey horse neighed impatiently across the street. Soft Spanish music rose from below while beyond the town the land swept brown and monotonous as far as the eye could see.

Lee took out his pipe, packed tobacco into it. He dreaded going downstairs, and for the hundredth time wondered why he was here. There was nothing between him and his father. After fifteen years, he wouldn't even recognize the man.

He held a match to the pipe, puffed thoughtfully. What a surprise to find Johnny in El Paso. Johnny'd always been a high roller, not the sort to settle in some hot, dry, sandy Texas border town. He had to watch Johnny. Five or six years ago Johnny had vowed to kill him. But after murdering Buford Mumford, Johnny'd been too concerned with saving his own hide to worry about anything else. Maybe he'd forgotten about Brandy Station.

The match burned Lee's fingertips, so he dropped it to the floor. He couldn't worry about Johnny. He had to face a real ghost. God, he hated it.

He left his room, walked downstairs, turned into the left-hand hall, and snailed to the last door on the right. He paused there, brown eyes almost black with concentration, then knocked on the door.

'Come on in.'

A tart taste filled Lee's mouth, but the time had come. He couldn't put it off any longer. He opened the door, stepped into the room and, closing the door, regarded the grey-fleshed countenance of the green-eyed man who watched him from the room's double bed. Hollow echoes lifted as Lee's leather heels tapped the floor between the door and the bed where he stared down into his father's shrunken cheeks and fever-scabbed lips.

'I don't think I know you,' those lips whispered.

'I'm Lee Keene.'

The fever-burned lips pulled tightly over yellow teeth. The emaciated head nodded. 'You look like your mother's people. Ruddy. Hawk-nosed. Slender. How old are you?'

'Twenty eight.'

'I ought to know, but I can't remember too well since I got the fever. I was afraid you wouldn't come.'

'I didn't want to come.'

'Another one of your mother's traits. She never lied about anything. Why did you come?'

'Ma wanted it that way.'

'She was a good woman. How is she?'

'Old and tired and worked out before her time, thanks to you.'

'You don't think much of your old daddy, do you boy?'

11

'Not much.'

'Well, at a time like this I reckon it don't matter. Drag up a chair.'

Lee placed a chair next to the bed, sank into it. He felt uncomfortable and didn't like it because he owed this man nothing. Not even respect. Still, he couldn't quiet the notion that he was being too hard. He puffed on his pipe, gaze returning to the pain-ravaged visage regarding him. His father had been a huge man. He had heavy bones and heavy shoulders plus a long frame. One big hand, now bones and veins, scuffed at hair almost as white as his pillow. Those green eyes looked weary, but they were alert and intelligent.

'How's the farm, boy?'

'We're making it.'

'I thought the war might have wiped you out. We've heard a lot about how the Yankees stripped the South.'

'You wrote so often we figured those stories must have upset you.'

Coughs shook the bed-ridden man who dabbed with a cloth at the red froth staining his lips. 'You don't give a man much room do you?'

'Only what I think he deserves.'

'And in your opinion George Keene

12

doesn't deserve much. Well, you're probably right. Pour me some of that whiskey, will you.'

'You allowed to drink?'

'No. But you can't kill a dead man. Pour it.'

Lee stood up, walked around the bed, and poured three fingers of bourbon into a glass. Before rounding the bed to regain his chair, Lee watched the old man gulp the whiskey eagerly. He fought the tide of pity rising in his throat. After what this man had done, he didn't deserve pity. Still, Lee had never been a hater, and he found it hard to hate now.

'So your ma sent you.'

'I already told you that.'

'You even wonder why I wanted to see you?'

'Nobody wants to die alone, and I wouldn't think you've made too many friends over the years.'

'In my business, you don't make *any* friends. That's one of the first things you learn. But that's not why I sent for you. I hit it, boy, I hit it big. Now it belongs to you and your mother, providing you've got the guts to bring it out.'

'I don't know what you're talking about.'

13

George Keene's gaze darted to the window, the closed door. He swallowed another swig of whiskey and, with a trembling hand, set the glass on the stand next to his bed. Then that hand searched under his pillow and withdrew a faded buckskin poke. Opening the poke, he shook five thumbnail-sized stones into his left palm. 'I'm talking about gold, boy. More than a man could spend in a lifetime.'

Lee drew slowly on the pipe. He was a slender, brown, straight-backed shape there in the chair, and smoke drifted up past his slim cheeks, past the crescent-shaped scar at the corner of his left eye. 'I'm not interested in your gold.'

'You're not interested in anything I've got are you?'

'That's a fact.'

'A while ago you were blowing off about how tired and worked-out your ma was. Here's the answer to all that. You can pay off that farm. Fix it so your ma can rest the remainder of her life. You interested in that?'

Lee puffed on the pipe, considered the floor between his shoes. He didn't see how he could accept anything from this man.

Not after all these years. He raised his head, gave his father a questioning look. 'After all this time, why didn't you leave us alone?'

George Keene swallowed more whiskey, replaced the glass on the stand. He closed his eyes, and the only sign of life in his grey visage was the breath whistling through his half-opened mouth. His shrunken face resembled a relief map with deep lines serrating his flesh into miniature frames. He coughed again and dabbed his lips with the red-spotted cloth as his eyes flickered open. 'You won't understand this, boy, but I meant to come back. I loved your ma. Still do. But I came out here to strike it rich. Your ma and me agreed that was the only way we could make it. That big strike was always over the next hill, and time just seemed to string out.'

The tobacco squeaked wetly in Lee's pipe and sludge embittered his mouth. He removed the pipe from his teeth, looked at the floor again.

A sigh escaped his father's lips. The bed creaked. 'I ain't gonna waste my energy. If you don't want to hear it, you might as well clear out.'

'I don't know. Maybe I owe it to Ma.'

'Ease over and check that hall. Then pour me another drink.'

Lee gave his father a curious look. He shrugged, stood up, and stepping to the door, opened it, and surveyed the empty hallway. He glanced back at the dying man, shook his head, and after closing the door, walked around the bed and refilled the whiskey glass.

After Lee regained his chair, George Keene rolled on his left side so that he faced his son. 'As you know, boy, I first tried my luck in California, but nothing turned up there. Then I heard about the Canyon de Oro legend. It seemed that back in sixteen hundred, Spanish soldiers brought a mule train out of Apache country. That train was loaded with gold. Apache gold. But that gold came from a sacred canyon, and the Apaches trailed those soldiers into Mexico. They trapped them somewheres in the Sierra Madres and slaughtered them. But not before the soldiers hid that shipment. The idea was for someone to get through to Chihuahua and bring back a relief party. Well, a man named Francisco Guzman got through, but he didn't return. He waited until he was sure all his companions were dead, after which he gathered up a band of *amigos* who planned to keep that gold for themselves.

'It didn't work out. They ran into bandits and were killed to the last man. But one of those men had told his sweetheart about the gold, so when they didn't return, she told everything. People been looking for that gold ever since, but nobody ever found it.

'Well, I ran into a fellow who supposedly pointed out the location. The two of us worked that range for six years, and the only thing we found was some rusty armour. Then Ken, that was the other fellow, gave it up. He figured our luck had run out, and I wasn't too sure he wasn't right. Still, I couldn't quit. I made trip after trip into that country and never found a thing. Then a few weeks ago, I stumbled on to it. Pure luck, boy. Nobody would have found it any other way. The map took me near the right location. I'd ridden by there a hundred times. So had lots of other folks, but they'd never found it either.'

George Keene coughed again, patted his lips with the cloth. He closed his eyes for a moment while heavy breath whistled past his dry lips. He opened his eyes, took a long sip of the whiskey, grimacing as he swallowed it. 'Give me a minute. Ain't strong enough to talk much anymore.'

Lee tapped out his pipe and ground the tobacco into the floor. He refilled the pipe and relit it. The old man seemed about finished. He had absolutely no color while the same red that brightened the rag streaked his eyes. Lee scratched his cheek. He tried to feel something for this shrivelled bag of bones. Pity. Remorse. But he couldn't. This man *was* his father. Nothing he'd done or hadn't done could alter that fact. Damn it. He ought to be able to feel something. At least shame for not feeling.

A series of coughs shook George Keene's huge, fleshless frame, and blood dribbled from the corners of his mouth. He wiped the blood away, forced down another swallow of whiskey. 'That gold is still there, boy. Enough to buy the whole state of South Carolina. You've got to bring it out. Otherwise all this has been for nothing.'

Lee considered the man's grey, grainy face. 'I don't know.'

'What's the matter? Ain't you got the backbone?'

'I can do anything you could do.'

'You may hate my guts, boy, but don't sell me short. That's rough country I'm talking about. Hot, not much water, Apaches, bandits, fever. A man's on his own. You're from the East. There's lots you don't know about things out here. You ever kill a man?'

'In the war.'

'I'm talking about looking a man dead in the eye and pulling the trigger.'

'No. I never did, nor do I want to.'

'Then I guess I'm talking to a boy about a man's job. Like I told you, I'm not the only one looking for that pot. Who knows you're in town?'

'The hotel clerk and Johnny Hughes.'

'If Bill Watson knows, the whole town knows. And Johnny Hughes. He's meaner than a sidewinder. You couldn't handle him. I guess you'd better climb on that coach and head back for the farm.'

'Maybe you're selling me short.'

'I doubt it.'

Lee's teeth cut into the pipe's stem. His stomach churned, and he felt his pulse quicken. He didn't like being called a coward. Not by a man who'd deserted his wife and only child. 'All right. I'll bring it out.'

'Your word to a dying man?'

'You got it.'

George chuckled. 'I see you've got your ma's temper. Let's just hope you've got her nerve. What I'm talking about ain't going to be easy. You'll have to beat everything I mentioned and more.'

'I said if you could, I can.'

A long shuddering breath tore past George Keene's lips. He closed his eyes again, brought the cloth to his mouth as a cough racked him. 'All I've got is this poke, a mule down at the livery, that shotgun in the corner, and the watch on the dresser. They're yours when I die. Sell the mule and the shotgun and tell everybody who asks you're headed home. Take the stage as far east as necessary to throw anyone following you off. Maybe Fort Hancock will do. That's only fifty miles from here, but if need be ride that coach all the way to South Carolina, work that farm for six months, then sneak back out here. You've got to throw everybody off your trail. And watch Johnny Hughes. He'd kill you for the fun of it. God knows what he'd do for that gold.'

'I know Johnny.'

'I reckon you do. I keep forgetting he's

from South Carolina. You'll find a map under the butt plate of that shotgun. Memorize it. Then burn it. The only map is to be in your head.' George Keene turned over on his back, sighed heavily. 'I'm tired, boy. We'll talk again later.'

Lee watched the green eyes close, knew they'd stay closed for a while this time. The old man was beat out. He couldn't live much longer. Funny, but that seamed face looked at peace. An easy breathing lifted that bony chest. Lee stood up as smoke drifted from his pipe. Looking down at his father, he realized the old devil had tricked him. He didn't want any part of that gold, but he'd given his word and saw no way out of it. He should never have come here despite his mother's pleading. He wanted no part of anything this man had to offer, for it would be tainted. Tainted with his mother's workworn hands and weary expression. That gold couldn't make her young again, nor could it erase his bitterness. Hell, he already had that farm back on the road to recovery. He didn't need help, and none had been available when he had needed it. He walked out of the room feeling trapped and angry.

21

It was cooler in the cantina, and loud voices filled the room. The odors of whiskey, leather and sweat mingled with the odors of tobacco and fried food, and Lee's nostrils twitched at the combination of smells. He found a spot at the bar where he ordered bourbon and repacked his pipe. The saloon was jammed with cowboys, vaqueros, men in business suits, and white-shouldered women.

He couldn't understand why Johnny had greeted him so warmly, for they'd never liked each other. They'd grown up near the same town, but they'd come from different sides of the social spectrum. Lee had been the son of a dirt farmer while Johnny had been a member of the planters' class. He'd had money, background and education.

While Johnny had hunted foxes, fought duels and danced with southern belles, Lee had hunted possum, fought the soil, and handled recalcitrant mules. In that South before the war, there'd been three classes of people: the landed gentry, the white trash, and the black slaves. As a member of the gentry, Johnny had regarded Lee in much the same fashion he regarded the blacks who farmed his father's land and groomed his horses.

The war had arrived, and they'd both joined Jeb Stuart's cavalry unit. Johnny, of course, had been an officer and, by the conflict's end, Lee had earned sergeant stripes. They'd fought side by side at Brandy Station, at Chancellorsville, and at Yellow Tavern where General Stuart had been mortally wounded. Their mutual antagonism had come into the open at Brandy Station. Johnny's command had captured a squad of bluecoats, and with the battle raging, he'd decided he had no time to waste on prisoners. He'd ordered those bluecoats shot, and when Lee had balked, he'd been severely reprimanded. Those bluecoats had been murdered anyway. Lee had turned in a report concerning the incident to General Stuart, but Johnny had talked his way out of a court martial. He'd sworn to kill Lee for betraying him; then, Lee had been transferred, and they'd not met again until the war ended.

Back home, Johnny had encountered more pressing problems than Lee. Buford Mumford, a turncoat who'd joined in Yankee scallawag schemes to appropriate southern farmland, had made the mistake of filing on Hughes Point, Johnny's old homestead. The loss of the Point had jolted

Johnny's father so badly, he'd suffered a fatal heart attack; whereupon, Johnny had hunted Buford down and put a bullet between his eyes. That killing had finished Johnny in South Carolina. With a Yankee warrant for murder plus a thousand dollar dead or alive reward, Johnny had only one option. Run. And so here he was in El Paso.

Lee laid his smoked-out pipe on the bar and sampled the whiskey. It was rotgut that burned a trail from his tongue to his belly, and the food would probably taste just as bad. The longer he was in Texas the more he wanted to go home, but the old man had pushed him into a corner. He'd have to live with this country for a few weeks no matter how much he disliked it.

'How's George?'

Lee glanced left to see Johnny Hughes settle against the bar. Johnny shoved his planter's hat to the back of his head, thrust his thumbs in the pockets of his fancy vest. A cigarette dangled from the corner of his mouth, and his blue eyes gleamed cheerfully. Lee shrugged. 'Not good. I don't think he'll last much longer.'

'I'm surprised he's lasted this long.

He was in bad shape when he pulled in here. Of course, we don't have a doctor.'

'Let me buy you a drink.'

'Sure. Good to see you again. Good to see anyone from back home. This is a hell of a country, isn't it.'

Lee waved the bartender over, ordered Johnny a drink. 'How long you been in El Paso?'

'About a year. The gambling's good and not much law to bother you. I guess you're glad to see your dad.'

'Not particularly.'

Johnny's eyebrows lifted. 'Like that, huh.'

'He walked out on us fifteen years ago. He could have been dead for all we knew.'

'Maybe you're being too hard on him. Obviously he didn't forget, or you wouldn't be here.'

'He wanted someone to bury him.'

Johnny rolled a sip of bourbon around in his mouth and regarded Lee shrewdly. 'I figured he meant to hand you that Canyon de Oro gold. Everybody knows he was looking for it.'

'He's been looking for gold most of

his life. Far as I know, he never found any.'

'Shame. Long trip out here for nothing.'

'Too long. I got a farm to work.'

Johnny finished his bourbon, rolled another cigarette, and stuck it in his mouth. 'He's your father, Lee. You ought to forget the past.'

'I can't. He put a terrible load on my ma. It made an old woman out of her.'

'Try to see it his way. He had the fever. He couldn't help what he was doing.'

'The fever?'

'Gold Fever. Lots of people get it, but I never knew anybody had it as bad as George. It was in his blood. He couldn't control it.'

'You seem to know a lot about it.'

'We've talked. I know how he felt about you and your mother. He wanted to strike it big for you.'

'I don't want to hear about it. I'll bury him, and that's all I owe him.'

'None of my business. Well, I got to find a game. This is Saturday and there's money in town. Don't play cards with me, Lee. I cheat.' With that, Johnny grinned and swaggered back to one of the tables.

Lee stared down into his glass. George, Lee couldn't refer to him any other way, had been right. Johnny thought George had located that gold and wanted to pass on the information to his son. But it wouldn't be hard to fool this town. Johnny would repeat what he'd been told, and when these people saw Lee aboard the stage coach, they'd believe it. He'd get the gold all right; not that it changed anything. Despite what Johnny said, Lee couldn't forgive the man who'd once been his father. Too much had happened.

Outside the sun set low on the horizon. The heat had diminished although a hot breeze swept the street. Lee noted the town was emptying even though horses, buckboards, and men and women still cluttered the thoroughfare. The land looked softer now; the skyline less bleak.

Lee ankled over the few feet separating the cantina from the hotel and entered the lobby. Hunger cramped his stomach, so he entered the hotel restaurant where he dined on steak, potato, canned apple pie, and coffee. With a fresh bowl of tobacco burning in his pipe, he approached the stairs and, as his shoe hit the first step, he paused reflectively. His gaze followed the hallway leading to George Keene's room. Perhaps he should drop by for a moment. When he returned to South Carolina, his mother would ask questions.

The door to George's room was ajar, and Lee pushed it open. From the doorway, he saw the blood soaking the man's nightshirt, and three quick steps carried him to the bedside. He touched the big artery at the side of George's throat but found no pulse. The blood had seeped from a hole in George's chest, an inch-long gash made by a knife. Lee's gaze leaped to the corner. When he spotted the shotgun leaning against the wall, he spun around the bed, snatched it up and, turning it barrel down, opened his Barlow, undid the screws, and lifted the plate from the gun's wooden butt. A folded paper lay snugly in the hollowed out contour.

Shoving the paper into his pocket, Lee replaced the metal plate and leaned the shotgun against the wall. Then he quick-stepped back to the bed and gazed down into the dead man's slack countenance.

Somehow that huge frame didn't look so big in death. There didn't appear to have been any struggle. If it hadn't been for all that blood, Lee would have sworn the old man was sleeping peacefully. He felt good about that. In the war, he'd seen too many faces shapeless with pain.

He turned to the dresser where he picked up the watch that was now his. It was a Waltham with a heavy gold chain and toggle bar. He flipped open the hinged metal cover. Inside that cover was a faded tintype of his mother holding a baby. He stared at the picture which suddenly blurred before he snapped the hinge and thrust the watch into his pocket.

He walked back to the bed where he gazed down at the dead man. His hand closed over a bony shoulder and, although he stared at the bed, he saw nothing. He stood there a long moment, a hook-nosed, brown-complexioned man whose rectangular face set thin-lipped and grim-cheeked. Abruptly, he wheeled from the bed, grabbed the shotgun, and marched from the room. He had a promise to keep. A debt to settle. And fifteen years of resentment to repay.

2

As the stage driver yelled, 'Fort Hancock', Lee considered the other passengers. To his left sat a young Mexican woman in a pearl-grey, neck-high dress. Black hair fell to her shoulders, and she seemed untouched by the heat and dust. She had good features: a high forehead, full lips, high cheekbones, and a pug nose. Across from Lee, a stubby rancher argued with his overweight wife while next to them a drummer who'd been on the coach when it pulled into El Paso gnawed at his thumbnail.

The coach swayed to a halt. The driver jumped to the ground, and boots scuffed over dirt as he hoofed to the rear of the coach. Wood squealed against wood, and a muffled oath reached Lee's ears. The young woman opened the door and stepped into the street, but Lee held his position waiting to see what the other passengers would do. When none of them moved, Lee shouldered from the coach.

Fort Hancock was a jumble of adobe houses, and out to his right Lee saw a square of building that constituted the fort. The driver swung up on the box where he handed Lee his black valise and a second portfolio that obviously belonged to the young woman. Then the driver kicked the team into motion, and dust spurted as the coach lurched east.

As Lee heeled around, his gaze caught the hazy outline of the Sleeping Woman Mountain. It didn't look like a six-day ride, but out here distance was confusing. He picked up the suitcases and walked over to where the woman stared southward.

'Anything wrong, ma'am?'

Soft brown eyes met his. Her shoulders lifted, fell. 'I don't know. My brother was supposed to meet me.'

Lee nodded at the stage office. 'Why don't we ask inside,' and carrying the valises led the way into the one-roomed affair.

A bald-headed man glanced up from his desk. 'Help you folks?'

The woman moistened her lips. 'My name is Aurora Lopez. My brother was to arrive from Casa Grandes yesterday. Perhaps he left a message?'

31

The bald-headed man stood up. He shook his head. 'We haven't had any strangers through here for days.'

Aurora seemed surprised, but she was a very self-contained young woman, and that willowy figure contained a tough, resilient core that Lee hadn't suspected.

Lee took her elbow again. 'You go on to the boarding-house. I'll see that your bag gets there.'

'Thank you. You've been kind.'

After arranging for the bags to be delivered, Lee marched over to Clarke's Mercantile. Inside, the smells of coffee and sugar and spices permeated the room, and a pot-bellied, bearded fellow nodded at Lee from behind the counter. Lee took a piece of paper from his coat pocket, handed it across the counter. 'Here's a list of things I'll need. I'll be wanting a horse and a mule also. Can you supply them?'

'I can supply anything you can pay for.'

'I'll want all this stuff come daybreak.'

'I'll have the mule loaded.'

'How far is it to Casa Grandes?'

'About a hundred miles.' The bearded man glanced at the list, pursed his lips. 'Going after that Canyon de Oro gold, I take it.'

32

'I didn't say anything about gold.'

'You didn't have to. Nobody goes to Casa Grandes with a month's supplies for any other reason. Stranger in these parts, ain't you?'

'Uh huh.'

The storekeeper plucked a cigar from a can, lighted it. He shook out the match, looked Lee up and down. 'Ain't none of my business, but you sure you know what you're getting into?'

'I can't honestly say I do.'

'Thought so. Well, rumors about gold spread for long distances, and that rumor has had over two hundred years to circulate. Lot of men been down in those mountains looking for that cache, but nobody ever brought any dust back that I know of. I suppose you know about the curse?'

'I hadn't heard that part of it.'

'When the Spaniards hauled that load out of Arizona, an Apache medicine man swore it would never reach Mexico City. He also swore that any white man who put a hand on it would die a violent death. Like I said, I've never seen any dust from that cache, but like rumors about the gold, there's rumors that more than one man has located it and every one of them's died.'

'I'm not much on superstition.'

'Neither am I, but a man don't have to be superstitious to realize the dangers of bringing gold out of those mountains. You not only have the Apaches to worry about, but the bandits. That land's nothing but rock and sand. I guess there's some water out there, but away from the rivers, it's in short supply.'

'Like I said, I'm going to Casa Grandes. I'll need some clothes and a pistol plus a Henry rifle and a shotgun. If things are as bad as you claim, give me about forty rounds for each. I'll take the clothes and handgun now.'

Lee left the store with two shirts, two pairs of pants, work boots, and a wide-brimmed hat. Feeling foolish, he stuffed the revolver into his waistband. He was no pistol shot, but everyone out here seemed to carry one, and it might come in handy. He wanted to look as though he belonged and hoped the new clothes and handgun would turn the trick.

At Newsome's boarding-house, he was greeted by a grey-haired, dumpy woman who said, 'Call me Ma. Everybody does. The room is fifty cents a night. Bath's a dime extra. Your room's the third door down the hall. Your valise is already in there.'

Figuring this might be his last bath for a long time, Lee forked out two quarters and a dime and was directed to the bath house. A splinter of a man, who called himself Mister Newsome, filled the tub with cold water and, after handing Lee a towel and a bar of soap, left the room. Lee undressed and relaxed in the tub. This was the first time he'd had a chance to think since yesterday, for he'd been busy arranging the funeral and selling the shotgun and mule. He'd studied the map last night before tucking it into his watch case. He'd spend some more time with it later, fully memorize it, then burn it. He couldn't help wondering if he was doing the right thing. He was needed at the farm, and he had to admit that he wasn't too keen on riding south.

Both George and that storekeeper had been frank about the dangers. As George had said, maybe he wasn't the man for the job. Hell, he was a farmer. His world consisted of soil and water and crops. Not one of rock and sandy desolation. He didn't know the first thing about Indians

35

and even less about bandits. What if he had to kill somebody! He'd killed in the war, but it wasn't the same as looking a man in the eyes and shooting him. He wasn't too sure he wouldn't hesitate when hesitation would be fatal. He should have stayed back East where he belonged. He had no business out here.

Promptly at six, he appeared at the dining-table; for Ma Newsome had explained that supper was served on time, and those who were late missed the meal. Aurora was already seated at the table conversing in Spanish with a weatherbeaten man of about forty sitting to her right. Two men in ranching clothes sat opposite her while the splintery Mister Newsome occupied the end chair. Lee said, 'Good evening', and settled in between the ranchers. The meal consisted of fried steaks, beans, squash, coffee and was followed by a large helping of chocolate cake.

After congratulating Ma Newsome on a fine supper, Lee ambled outside and, dropping into one of the six chairs scattered across the porch, filled his pipe and lit it. The sun had faded beyond the horizon, but a full moon lightened the street. The wind had died while the fierce heat had been replaced by a comfortable coolness.

The screen door opened and Aurora stepped onto the porch. She smiled and walked over to stand by the chair next to his. 'I want to thank you again for what you did today.'

Lee smiled back. 'I'm glad I could help.'

She glanced at the street, and in the moonlight her profile was slim and flawless. She had replaced the grey dress with a calico outfit that moulded her full breasts and slender waist, and Lee reflected again that Aurora was a beautiful woman with poise and breeding. She had an easy, frank style, a friendliness that drew men to her; yet, her demeanor spoke louder than words that it was only friendliness, nothing more. Aurora would never worry that a man might step out of line. That line, although intangible, was too apparent for even a fool to mistake.

'Do you mind if I join you?' she said.

'Glad to have company.'

'I could tell by your clothes that you're a long way from home. One does get lonely.'

'One does,' he admitted. 'Things are so

37

different out here.'

'I love this country. I wouldn't want to live anywhere else.'

'Too flat and dry for me. I like trees, grass, water.'

'I suppose the land is monotonous, but it has its own special beauty.'

Smoke rose from his pipe as he considered the foreground. 'At night it's beautiful. Everything seems softer. During the day, everything is so stark.'

She turned to him, and he could see the white line of her teeth as her full lips parted. 'I understand you're looking for the Canyon de Oro gold.'

'I never said that.'

'This is a small town. Everyone knows you're headed for Casa Grandes, and no one goes there unless they live there or use it as a stop-over between here and the Sierra Madres. You are after the gold.'

'I understand it's there for the taking.'

'True, but I'm not interested in gold. I'm interested in reaching Casa Grandes. I want to ride with you.'

He took the pipe from his mouth, regarded her gravely. 'That's impossible.'

'Why?'

'It's too dangerous. I can't take the responsibility.'

'I'm not asking you to take the responsibility. I have to reach Casa Grandes, Mister Keene.'

'Call me Lee.'

'Lee, I won't be a burden. As a matter of fact, I can be of help. I know how to ride and shoot. If anything happens, you might be glad I'm there.'

'I'm sure I would, but I still can't take the responsibility. Try to understand.'

'Do you speak Spanish?'

'No.

'Then you need me.'

'The answer's no. I'm sorry.'

'I guess there's no more to say. Thank you again for your kindness. Good night.'

After his pipe smoked down, he knocked the tobacco into a flower bed. As he straightened, a thought hit him. Aurora had said that everyone in town knew his destination, and George had warned him that he must keep his comings and goings secret. A lot of people wanted that gold. They'd do anything to get it. Lee stuck the empty pipe in his mouth, sucked at it reflectively. He had to be on guard tomorrow, had to be certain no one followed him. Aurora's request had been a stroke of luck. He hadn't considered that Fort Hancock's storekeeper might be a source of danger. He'd have to be more careful, for by nature he was a friendly, open individual. This job called for someone observant, restrained, and noncommittal.

Back in his room, he lit the lamp and set it on the table opposite the open window. He pulled out the Waltham, opened the case, and removed the folded square of white paper. The faded tintype stared back at him. He knew a sudden sadness and understood that all these years he'd been wrong. George... No, his father hadn't forgotten. As Johnny Hughes had said, he'd been too hard on the man, but it was fourteen years too late to make amends. Fourteen years of anger and waste. He'd never known his father, and his father had never known him, but he knew now that for his father those had been lonely years. Years in which he'd missed his family; yet, years in which something he couldn't control had driven him. Lee closed the watch case. If he ever had a son, nothing would come between them.

Sitting down at the desk, he unfolded

the map. He had already memorized most of the important details. The spot to head for on the Sleeping Woman range. The four trails rippling south-east. The river. The waterfall. All he needed to do before destroying the map was be certain he knew the location of the water-holes between here and the mountains.

He removed the empty pipe from his mouth and, absentmindedly, lay it on the edge of the table. It was too near the edge and toppled to the floor. As he bent over to retrieve it, something breezed by his ear. Something that made a thudding noise as it struck the wall. His gaze rocketed up to where a knife's hilt quivered above the table, and his gaze shot to the window where he saw a pale visage jerk back into the night. Slamming to his feet, he leaped to the window from where he saw a bulky form sprint toward the corral behind the stage coach office.

His boots pounded the floor as he raced for the bed and scooped the revolver from beneath his pillow. He grabbed the map, crushed it into a wad that he thrust into his pocket, and rammed back to the window. He saw nothing but open land, the corral, three houses scattered haphazardly to his left and understood that chase was useless.

Striding back to the table, he yanked the knife from the wall. It was an ordinary Bowie that could have belonged to anyone. He hefted the knife in his hand wondering who'd thrown it, wondering how they'd known who he was, and wondering if it was the same knife that had killed his father. Someone knew he had the map, for otherwise to kill him closed the trail to that Apache gold. He jammed the pistol into his waistband and pulled the map from his pocket. He knew it well enough. It was time to destroy it.

3

Lee looked at his Waltham. Nine o'clock. He'd been on the trail almost three hours. Even this early in the day, heat had begun to cage this land. He glanced back at his mule, patted his black stallion's flank. The storekeeper had provided him with good animals. He might be a greenhorn in this country, but he knew horses and mules. A lifetime on the farm had taught him that.

His gaze lifted and he saw a slender figure far in the distance. He'd noticed that rider an hour earlier, so this sighting solidified the fact that someone followed him. Up ahead this country fed into smooth hillocks while, beyond, more rugged terrain flowed westward. Once he reached those hills, he planned to find out who trailed him. Maybe it would be someone who owned a bone-handled Bowie.

He swung to the front and clucked the big horse forward. Whoever trailed him didn't give him much credit, for the man made little effort to remain out of sight. It was his good fortune that his pursuer underestimated him. He hadn't spent four years in the cavalry for nothing. He knew how to lay down a false trail, double back and plan an ambush. In another hour or so, he'd have that fellow in his rifle sights. Then he would get the answers to some of the questions bothering him.

Far in the distance, the Sleeping Woman range spread out in a north and south direction. From Casa Grandes, he'd head straight for her navel. The rest would be easy. He'd load this mule and in three weeks be swinging aboard an east-bound stage at Fort Hancock. He dreaded bringing bad news to his mother. She'd never stopped loving her husband despite all the toil, the despair and the loneliness he'd caused her. Lee had to admit that she'd known his father far better than he. It had taken that faded tintype to make him admit that the man still cared; whereas, his mother had never doubted it.

A flock of quail winged overhead. Some purple flowers carpeted the ground under the horse's hooves while clumps of cactus jutted up from the surrounding sands. To Lee, this was a no-man's land. He was amazed that anything grew here. He couldn't get accustomed to all this empty space, and he wished again for the green hills of home.

Glancing back, Lee saw the solitary figure holding his distance. He couldn't understand how anyone knew about him. The only person to alight from the stage at Fort Hancock had been Aurora, and he'd been seated so that he would have seen anyone following the coach. This region had no telegraph; no way for anyone to flash word from El Paso to Fort Hancock. Yet, word had passed. Otherwise the attempt on his life made no sense. The knife had been hurled for one reason only. Somebody wanted that map.

The land changed from yellow flats to brown hills, and the sun boiled down causing heat waves to dance in the distance. No trees broke the horizon which had a scanty covering of grass and sagebrush, while the smells of dust and sweaty cotton and sweaty leather pressed in on him.

Far off to the left a hawk floated. Suddenly the hawk spotted its prey and flashed downward in a dive that ended when the hawk scooped up some terrified reptile and winged into the distance. Upon reflection, Lee decided that life in the West was symbolically stated in that act. Back East, the law and the courts protected one's rights, and public opinion pressured a man to forego certain actions. In the West, there was no law or judicial system. The strong fed on the weak, for a man could commit any deed he was strong enough to back up, and public opinion seemed to support such activity. A man had to depend on himself, and what he was had to surface.

Lee urged the stallion into a trot, knowing full well that he left a clear trail. He paralleled those hills for roughly an hour, then swung the black behind one of the mounds and dismounted. Uncertain of his animals, he hobbled them before slipping his rifle from its scabbard. A quick look revealed that his pursuer had not yet reached the rounded hillocks, and Lee scampered back a good hundred yards where he located a forked, dugout-like indentation in a hillside. From here he was shielded from the rider dogging his tracks; yet, he'd have a clear line on his follower when he jogged by.

The sun burned from its zenith, and sweat gathered under Lee's hatband. The new clothes felt stiff and his chest and back began to itch. He stuck the empty pipe into his teeth and sucked on it for comfort. Soon he heard muffled hoofbeats, and his mouth went dry as those hoofbeats grew more pronounced. His hands perspired while a hollow spot formed below his breastbone. He nestled deeper into the dugout while his thoughts pictured one scenario after another. What if the man made a fight of it! What if he refused to heed the advice to find some other trail! What if he was only another traveler headed for Casa Grandes! Lee shook his

46

head. How in the hell could he know? Then he remembered Aurora's statement. No one traveled to Casa Grandes unless he lived there or was seeking Apache gold.

Horse hooves thumped distinctly now. Lee wiped his right hand on his shirt front, settled his rifle barrel into the V between his thumb and forefinger. A horse's head shoved into view, and Lee held his breath as the rider edged into his line of sight. As he thumbed back the rifle's hammer, its metallic click jerked the rider's head in his direction.

He stared directly into Aurora Lopez's shocked face. When she saw him, her lids closed, then opened as relief slackened her features. He eased the hammer forward and rose to his feet. His lips pulled into a short grimace, and he shook his head again. 'You ought to know better than to follow a man like this.'

'There was no other way to follow you.'

'What if I'd shot you?'

'Why should you do that? Obviously, I meant you no harm.'

'It wasn't obvious to me. Not after last night.'

'What's so different about last night?'

'Someone tried to kill me.'

Her mouth formed a loose O. Then she glanced down at her hands as some furtive expression tunneled over her complaisant visage. 'I didn't know.'

'What are you doing out here anyway?'

'I told you I had to get to Casa Grandes.'

'And I told you not with me.'

She shrugged, a movement that lifted the full breasts under the hickory shirt. A smile tugged at her lips, and her eyes slanted good-humoredly. A brown Stetson capped her thick, brown hair and she wore black pants stuffed into stovepipe boots. This casual attire was a far cry from the stiff, formal, high-necked dresses she'd worn yesterday; it gave a new dimension to her beauty.

'You can turn that mare in the opposite direction.'

'Then I'd be going the wrong way.'

'I'm not taking you with me.'

'This is the only way to Casa Grandes. Can I help it if we're riding the same trail?'

'There is no trail.'

'Casa Grandes is dead ahead. How would you have me get there?'

'Safely. And for that you need escort.'

'But you said you wouldn't take me.'

'You know what I mean. Get in touch with your people. Let them send someone to accompany you.'

'I need to get there now.'

Breath bubbled between Lee's clenched teeth. What did a man do with a hardhead like this! She meant to dog his tracks regardless, and there wasn't much he could do about it. He glanced at her determined countenance. She might appear sweet and manageable, but underneath that easygoing surface lay a resourceful, gritty, impetuous nature. Last night when she'd so gracefully accepted his refusal, she'd intended to follow him, planning to catch up when he was too far from the border to send her back. 'All right. I know when I'm beat. Let me pick up my animals.'

Soon they rode side by side with the Sleeping Woman Range looming solidly before them. Aurora was a first-class horsewoman. She sat the saddle like she was glued there. At least she hadn't lied about her ability to ride. She wore a gunbelt, and a rifle's butt jutted from its scabbard. He wondered if she'd told the truth when she'd said she could shoot, but considering all that had happened, he felt no need to doubt her.

At noon they halted near a clump of creosote brush whose yellow flowers seemed to wilt under the sun. They ate biscuits and fried bacon that Ma Newsome had provided, afterwards washing the sandwiches down with 'airtight' tomatoes. He packed his pipe, fired up, and they were back in the saddle with the brown hills closing off the country behind while they followed a dry riverbed that led into the rockier terrain ahead.

They rode steadily until dusk softened the countryside and pulled up for the night at a rectangular water-hole he remembered from the map. He unsaddled both horses, pulled the packs from the mules and hobbled the animals. After gathering an armload of firewood, he hunkered down by the water-hole.

He puffed at the pipe, gaze on the willowy shape fronting him. Her eyes were shadowed by the hat brim, but he could see the curve of her lips, the roundness of her lower face. 'I wonder what your people would think if they knew you were out here with a stranger?'

'They'd be worried.'

'Tell me about your family. Your life.'

Her shoulders seemed to stiffen while her arms tightened around her knees.

'I'm not prying. Just passing time.'

'You mean you haven't made up your mind about me?'

'I've got some ideas.'

'What are they?'

'I've spent my life on the other side of the fence from people with property and money. I think you belong on their side.'

Her head dipped, and when it lifted, a smile parted her full lips. 'You must be a good judge of people.'

'I've always thought so.'

'You're right about me. My life has been parties and dancing and flirting with young men. I didn't know it showed.'

'It's pretty obvious that you're a person of quality.'

Her head dipped again, and a long silence ran between them. When her head lifted, her lips compressed tightly as her fingers opened and shut in slow rhythm. 'Good night,' she said and, unfolding her hands and legs, lay on her side, face away from him.

Smoke raveled up across Lee's face, and his thoughts reshuffled the events of the last few days. Who would have thought he could overcome the disdain he'd so long felt for his father! Who would have thought he would end up in the middle of nowhere with this headstrong, beautiful girl? Life was a chart, deceptive and uncertain. What had gone before only made a man wonder what was yet to come, but he had no desire to be a prophet. Life involved too many ups and downs, and the down ones were better off not knowing. So thinking, he knocked out the pipe and sank back on his bedroll.

Morning found them riding a trail leading through rockbound gullies that fed into tablelands of igneous rock pushing into canyons and draws, wild and silent. Heat gathered in these lower regions, and the breeze that cooled the mesas interlocking these formations of wind-turned rock felt refreshing. At noon they halted in a wide gulch where yellow stone and iron grey soil formed a flat bottom land.

'Coffee now?' Lee asked.

'I think so.'

While Lee gathered wood, Aurora unpacked the coffee pot and poured water into it from a canteen. Lee lit a fire, set the coffee pot in the flames, and squatted with his arms over his thighs waiting for the water to boil.

Aurora's gaze darted around the campsite. 'What was that?'

'I didn't hear anything.'

'I did.'

'Imagination.'

Her gaze searched the clearing as her forehead bunched with concern. Head cocked slightly, she listened intently, then gave a little shrug. 'I guess so.'

When the water boiled, Lee threw in a handful of coffee. Then he leaned back on one elbow waiting for the grounds to boil. The sky was a blue lake without one cloud to break its surface. The animals browsed in the background and, far ahead, the lofty peaks of the Sierra Madres lined the horizon. Lee sucked at the empty pipe. It was hot here but peaceful. They'd made good time.

A flurry of small wings broke the stillness as a covey of cactus wrens shot upward. Lee pushed to a sitting position, and across the fire, he saw surprise and apprehension slim Aurora's cheeks. He looked to his right as five men edged into the gully.

They wore broad-brimmed sombreros while the bandoleers criss-crossed their chests. Their leader, a wiry fellow with an ugly purple scar angling down his left cheek, wore a dirty charro outfit. Two revolvers were belted around his waist. Next to him stood a man about Lee's height with a heavy black beard, brown eyes and a blank expression. At black-beard's elbow, a potbellied, flabby-visaged individual dug at his teeth with a thumbnail while his cunning little eyes blinked at Aurora. The third fellow was a youngster whose beardless cheeks and boyish countenance served as a sharp contrast to the lust sharpening his gaze. The final member, whose tired eyes and grizzled complexion reflected boredom, looked about fifty.

The tall fellow with the scar flashed a smile that revealed tobacco-stained teeth. *'Que pasa?'*

Lee glanced at Aurora whose hand clutched her throat. He saw the terror in her eyes, the rigid expression that fought to keep that terror from reaching her sensitive face. 'What did he say?'

'Call me Raul. I speak English,' the scar-cheeked one answered. 'I wondered what you were doing here. Don't you know this is dangerous country, full of bandits and Apaches?'

Lee glanced at Aurora again; then, he met the scar-faced man's crafty gaze, 'My wife and I are headed for Casa Grandes.'

The scar-faced Mexican chuckled. 'Casa Grandes. A fine town. I know it well.'

Lee heard his teeth grind and he knew a fearful desperation. The Mexicans had fanned out around the gully and, as Lee's gaze ticked off each hardened visage, he felt his stomach shrink. These men were animals with no conception of mercy. Lee groped for a way out of this and found none. He had a pistol in his waistband, but he would never reach it. His only chance lay in talk, while the chill spreading from the base of his neck to the tip of his spine told him talk was useless.

The fat man belched. He scratched his bulging belly while his pig eyes undressed Aurora. The older fellow stroked his mustache. The young one stared expectantly at his scar-faced leader while the black-bearded bandit pulled at one ear.

Scarface drew a finger down the purple scar tissue. 'You are lucky we found you. This is bandit country.'

'Yeah. Lucky,' Lee said.

The bandit leader's gaze bracketed Lee

while his tongue licked at his lower lip. 'I think you should give me your pistol.'

Lee shrugged, pulled the revolver from his waistband, and handed it to the scar-faced bandit.

The grizzled old-timer shuffled over to Lee. 'Maybe we should find out what he's carrying.'

Lee's lips clicked together. He reached inside his shirt and handed over his poke.

The bearded man opened the poke, shook some nuggets into his hand. *'Caramba!'*

Scarface hustled over to his companion. He snatched the poke from the other man's hand, stared down into its open neck. His gaze shifted to Lee for a moment. 'You two come with us. My *jefe* will want to talk with you.'

4

The tabletop was roughly 200 yards wide and 500 yards long. Directly off to the right was a corral of still green timbers, and the odors of hay and manure rode out from this area. Horses of every color and description ranged inside the corral, and a man in rolled-up trousers and a red undershirt soaked his feet in a brook welling out of the ground nearby.

Fifty yards to the front, Lee counted six more men sprawled on serapes and blankets. These men cleaned rifles and saddle gear. They glanced curiously at Lee and Aurora. Two huge, smoke-blackened pots hung over a fire, and beyond the fire Lee saw four tents. Twenty feet from these tents, a single tent squatted and through the rolled-up sidings Lee saw a heavy-set individual seated at a table. A woman stepped from one of the tents. She approached the cooking pots and dumped in some red meat. A woman's laugh drifted from one of the other tents, and a rider rumbled in from the west, his horse dragging a sled of firewood. Lee gave whoever selected this location his due. The area was ringed with solid rock with its front entrance facing the convoluted trail Raul had followed; the rear entrance, which Lee had not pin-pointed, was probably as difficult to navigate. With well-placed lookouts, this place could never be overrun.

Raul halted near the corral. 'Jaime, take care of the horses.' He motioned to Lee and Aurora. 'You two, walk to the big tent.'

Lee led the way across the tabletop. As they passed the men lying on the blankets, one of them said something in Spanish and the others laughed. Lee kept his gaze to the front. He didn't have to understand Spanish to understand what he'd just heard.

As they approached the tent, the man at the table swung in their direction. Surprise glittered in his eyes, but he said nothing as they stepped into the tent. Instead, he poured himself a shot of tequila from the bottle near his left elbow while his artful gaze probed Aurora's slender form.

Raul said, 'I have brought guests, *jefe.*'

The other man looked at Lee, and Lee sensed the cruelty behind that politic gaze. This man was big of shoulder and big of chest, and a mop of thick, black hair settled shaggily over his flaring ears. Confidence showed in his relaxed manner. His countenance was sleek with round, almost chubby, features, but it was a chubbiness remarkable for its lack of fat. He swallowed the tequila, belched, and patted his meaty lips. 'Where did you find them?'

'A few miles from here. They say they are going to Casa Grandes.'

'To Casa Grandes.'

Raul walked around to Lee's right. He reached inside his shirt and handed Lee's poke to his chief. 'We found this.'

The man at the table hefted the poke in his right hand. Then, he opened the draw strings and poured four nuggets into his palm. His dark eyes slanted up at Lee while his heavy lips parted in a smile. 'This is a lot of gold to be carrying in such dangerous country. What would happen if you ran into bandits?'

Lee's stomach muscles ridged as a chill touched his backbone. 'Why don't you tell me.'

The big man laughed. He drew a knife from his belt and jabbed it into the table. His gaze swept back to Aurora, and his smile froze in place as his eyes undressed her.

'They have a pack mule and many supplies. Enough for at least a month,' Raul said.

The *jefe* belched again as he reconsidered Lee. His lips pulled together as some furtive thought tunneled over his congenial face. He looked down at the dirt flooring; his broad forehead furrowed as his cheeks bunched in thought. 'So you are going to Casa Grandes?'

Lee nodded. He wondered what bothered the man. What had thrown him into this sudden concentration? 'My wife and I are visiting her parents.'

Raul grunted. His forefinger traced the ugly scar. 'With a pack animal plus a month's supplies. You lie.'

'I'm a stranger in this country. Why should I lie?'

The *jefe's* sleepy eyes considered Lee for another long moment. He scratched behind his right ear as a quizzical expression blunted his round cheeks. 'You say you are a stranger; yet, I know you from somewhere. Raul, doesn't he look familiar?'

'He looks like all gringos.'

'No. There is something...what is your name?'

'Lee Keene.'

The *jefe* threw back his head and laughed. 'Of course. Loco George. You are his son.'

Lee stared at Aurora, looked at the

grinning bandit chief. 'Loco George?'

'George Keene. He is your father. No?'

'That's a fact.'

'I am Manuel Ortega. I know your father well. For years he has searched this land for the Apache gold. You are welcome here.'

Raul snorted as Ortega stepped forward and grabbed both of Lee's shoulders. The man was so close that Lee could smell the garlic on his breath. Ortega's cheeks were slack with smiling, but Lee saw beneath that surface geniality. Beneath the amiability of Ortega's face, so dark it revealed his Indian heritage, lurked a will that lusted for power. It was a thirst so primitive that Ortega's carefully patented friendliness could never completely camouflage it. Ortega was a hard, brutal, crafty personality, made even more dangerous by his ability to play a part.

'How is your father?' Ortega said.

'He's dead.'

Ortega's eyelids closed down until his gaze was hidden from those fronting him. His politic countenance remained as bland as flour but the hands on Lee's shoulders slackened almost imperceptibly. 'I did not know. So Raul is right. You do look for gold.'

'If I can find it.'

'*Verdad,*' Ortega muttered. He turned to the table where he poured two glasses of tequila; then, he swung around and handed one of the glasses to Lee. 'To my old friend, your father, and to my new friend, his son.'

Lee's hand closed around the glass. He read the greed in Ortega's eyes. Sensed the evil lurking behind that agreeable visage; still, he lifted the glass in a salute and swallowed the contents. He had never drunk tequila and it tasted like mush, but he returned Ortega's smile as he handed him the empty glass.

Ortega nodded. He placed the glasses on the table and swinging over to Lee looped an arm around his shoulders. 'I must apologize for my men, but this is dangerous country. One must be on guard always.'

Lee forced back the disgust flooding him. He didn't like Ortega's smell, he didn't like Ortega's looks; and he didn't like Ortega's pretentious charm. He wanted to throw off Ortega's half-embrace and smash his offensive face. Instead, he shrugged disarmingly. 'Mistakes are made.'

'Mistakes are made. That is life.'

'Since you feel that way, I'm sure my wife and I can be on our way.'

'Of course. Of course. But it is late. You must be tired. Hungry. Tonight you and your wife shall have my tent. Now rest. We will eat later.'

Lee watched Ortega and Raul hoof out towards one of the other tents, and after they disappeared behind its closure, he heeled around to Aurora. Her dusty features sagged with strain and fatigue, but her brown eyes were alert and worried. 'Do you think he will keep his word?'

'I know he will. He wants that gold and thinks I'm fool enough to lead him to it.'

'You know where it is, don't you?'

'All that matters is that he believes I do. Are you all right?'

'If we get out of this, I will be.'

Lee packed his pipe, lighted it, and sat on the edge of the tent's single cot. The smoke stung his lips, but the tobacco soothed his frayed nerves. Somewhere down the line he'd throw Ortega on a false trail. He'd never dreamed he would ever again need the stratagems he'd mastered during the war, but the tricks he'd learned with Stuart's cavalry would enable him to cope with Ortega. He'd leave a clean trail from here to Casa Grandes; then, after he'd dropped Aurora, he'd cover his tracks so well Ortega would be riding in circles.

His gaze found Aurora who slumped wearily at the table. She'd had a terrible day, but she'd demonstrated a strength and resilience he'd never suspected. Despite the well-bred upbringing that showed in her posture, her voice, her aristocratic features, she was no spoiled brat. Aurora had stamina and nerve while beneath her natural grace lay a gritty, practical, resourceful nature that formed the core of her personality. He'd never met a woman he admired more, and sitting here looking at her lovely, responsive face, he realized he'd miss her when he rode out from Casa Grandes.

A jaybird's cry lifted from the stunted oaks lining the draw. The horses' hooves rang off stone, and a nine o'clock sun sent long shadows before them.

Aurora Lopez still couldn't believe that Ortega had released them. Twenty hours ago, she'd thought they were finished; yet, here they were safe and almost sound with freshly filled canteens, rested horses, and an open trail. She understood that more trouble with Manuel Ortega faced them, but Johnny Hughes would know how to handle it. He should overtake them soon, for he could read sign and would easily evade the same bandits that she and Lee had so stupidly allowed to surprise them.

She couldn't blame Lee. He was a tenderfoot who lacked the experience to understand the problems separating him from the gold he intended to pack out of this country. But she was a Texan who had spent her entire twenty-two years overcoming misfortune. She knew men like Manuel Ortega roamed this part of Mexico, so it had been her job to prevent an episode such as the one they'd endured. Johnny counted on her, and she had almost let him down. For her and Johnny, that gold solved everything. With it, they could live a decent life. A comfortable life. That gold meant an end to crooked gambling, cheap hotels, and, at times, compromise on her part. Still, life with Johnny had been far better than life before him. Now she need please only one man instead of many. Not that Johnny was that easy to please. He could be demanding, quarrelsome, even cruel, but since he could also be kind, considerate, and charming, she had learned to read his moods well enough to anticipate his outbursts and keep out of his way until those outbursts subsided.

The acrid odor of Lee's tobacco reached her. Her gaze considered him briefly, then edged back to the front. He was so unlike Johnny. Whereas Johnny was shrewd, Lee was naive. Whereas Johnny was vain, Lee was modest. Whereas Johnny was wild, Lee was restrained, and whereas Johnny had a definite mean streak, Lee was kind. They also had much in common. They were both courageous, confident, and intelligent, and they both shared an outgoing personality that everyone responded to. Because of these likenesses, they should have been friends, but Aurora knew that Johnny hated Lee. She didn't understand Johnny's hatred, but it had something to do with the war. They had served in the same unit where in some way Johnny had been betrayed. Johnny had never forgiven that betrayal. From what little she'd seen of Lee, she found it difficult to believe he'd betray anyone, but Johnny insisted.

'When do you think we'll reach Casa Grandes?' Lee said.

'Late tomorrow afternoon.'

5

Johnny Hughes reined in his palomino and took his first look at Casa Grandes. It was a typical Mexican town built so that it formed a square around the plaza. After the long, hot ride from the border, the late afternoon breeze felt refreshing while the tall oaks and sycamores threw a welcoming shade over the town.

He knee'd the palomino ahead and followed the street until he reached the stable where he dismounted and handed the reins to the stablehand. Dusting off his coat and pants, he angled for the cantina diagonally across the plaza from the stable. Soft guitar music strummed from the cantina accompanied by the lilting strains of 'La Paloma'. The spicy odor of chile reached out from the café, but Johnny ignored his hunger and shouldered into the bar.

The cantina seemed dark even though the shaded plaza had given his eyes relief from the trail's blinding glare. Water-filled jars hung from the ceiling, and the mingled smells of tequila, beer, and tobacco streaked the room. Johnny placed both hands on the bar. 'Whiskey.'

When the bartender set out a bottle and a glass, Johnny pulled a handkerchief from his hip pocket and wiped the dust from the glass. Eight or ten men lounged in the bar, and their animosity was as strong as the smells permeating this room. Johnny understood how most Mexicans felt about gringos, so he didn't let the hostility bother him. To show his contempt for this bunch of greasers, he lifted his glass in a mocking gesture that took in the guitar player and the singer, as well as the customers, downed his shot, poured another, and swallowed it.

Behind him the swinging doors squeaked, and he turned to see Lee Keene push into the room. Lee's pupils dilated; he hesitated, then ankled over to the bar.

'Bartender, another glass,' Johnny smiled.

Glass clicked against wood, but Lee ignored it. He took out his pipe, packed tobacco into it while a guarded expression thinned his cheeks.

Lee broke a match from a match block. He struck the match on the bar and with calculated deliberation passed the flame over the pipe. That guarded expression still closed off his thoughts, and the brief surprise that had jolted him at the doorway was now masked by a studied indifference. He dropped the match into a spittoon, expelled a streamer of smoke. 'What brings you to Casa Grandes?'

'I'm here for my health.'

'You don't look sick to me.'

'I'm running a high fever.'

'Gold fever?'

'You guessed it.'

'That seems to be a common malady in these parts.'

'I figured this might be the place to cure it.'

'I don't think you'll find any cure here.'

'I disagree. Frankly, I'm feeling better already.'

Johnny watched Lee's gaze drop to the floor. He puffed thoughtfully at the pipe, and little lines plowed out from his lip corners. Johnny followed Lee's thoughts as he ticked off, item by item, every move he'd made from El Paso to this barroom,

69

but Lee'd never put his finger on it. He was too much the southern gentleman to ever suspect Aurora.

Lee removed the pipe from his mouth, sipped his whiskey. 'How'd you find me?'

'Followed you.'

'Across this country?'

'Not too difficult when the trail's marked.'

'So that's it.'

'Lee, you never were a good judge of women.'

'I never realized I was that bad.'

'Where's Aurora?'

'Over at the hotel.'

'Guess I'll finish this drink and mosey on over. You want another one?'

'I'll buy my own.'

Johnny finished his drink, dropped a coin on the bar, and swaggered outside. His arrival had jolted Lee, but he stayed cool. Lee had even covered what had to be a big disappointment concerning Aurora. But Lee had always been level-headed. A little squeamish, perhaps, but never short of nerve. Johnny remembered the time he and Lee plus a dozen troopers had charged a Federal outpost near Burnsville. Lead had ripped the forest around them, and the Yankees had outnumbered them three to one. Some of the boys had showed yellow that afternoon, but not Lee.

Johnny shook his head regretfully. He'd hated to see those days end. He'd loved the war. In the South, a man in grey uniform could have anything he'd wanted. Especially if that man was an officer. He'd treasured every minute. The admiration, the respect, the glory showered by civilians. Those times had been good, but when he remembered the war, as he often did, he relived the fighting. Position and birth had made him a born leader, plus he'd had an instinct for making the right decisions. To lead a successful charge, to root out an enemy position, to bottle up retreating forces and destroy them left him with the inner glow that most men felt after several shots of ninety-proof bourbon. But most of all he'd enjoyed the killing. Nothing stimulated him more than the jar of a sword driving through flesh, the blank expression on an enemy face as the life drained from him, the frightened look in a Yankee's eyes just as a pistol exploded in his face. For Johnny, the smell of blood, sweat, and gunpowder had always produced an acute shock of exhilaration.

Yes, by God, he'd hated the news that General Lee had surrendered. Life had never been the same.

With disgust leaving an acerbic taste in his mouth, he hiked over the square. That he could have sunk to this. Trudging over a dusty square in a God-forsaken Mexican town to a Mexican trollop who believed he loved her. Christ! What a comedown. But the old life was still possible. Again there could be a huge white house, dozens of servants, good whiskey, fast horses, and beautiful women, and Lee Keene possessed the key to that lost world. Johnny shook his head. Of course, he could never return to Hughes Point. The moment he'd blown that sneering, arrogant, scallywag face into bloody goo any chance to regain the Point had ended. But there were other places. New Orleans, for example. To wear a decent suit of clothes, to escape this heat and dust, to talk with cultured people. Such had been his dream for years, and the time had finally come, but who would ever have imagined his opportunity would arrive in the person of Lee Keene? That the one man he so hated would be his salvation?

Reaching the hotel, he crossed the lobby

to the desk. 'I'm looking for Señorita Aurora Lopez.'

'Up the stairs to the right. Number eight.'

The stairs creaked under Johnny's weight, and he followed the hall until he found the number. He knocked three times and waited impatiently as footsteps skipped over the flooring. The door opened and Aurora's full lips parted joyfully. Her arms wrapped around his neck, and he submitted to her kiss while his mind sought the right words. Long ago, he'd tired of her, but she still had her uses. Admittedly, he owed her something; but that debt would soon be paid, and he would be rid of her plus the miserable existence he'd endured for so long.

She pulled him inside and closed the door. 'We ran into some bandits.'

'And you're alive?'

'Their leader was Manuel Ortega. He was a friend of Lee's dad.'

'I've heard of Ortega. He's a killer. I can't see him as anybody's friend.'

'Ortega knows about the gold.'

'How could he?'

'Lee had a poke full of nuggets on him.'

'Damn! That means Ortega will be

watching every move we make. I should have kept that poke.'

'You knew about it?'

'What about the map?' Johnny said, ignoring her question.

'What makes you so certain Lee has a map?'

'Don't worry. I know.'

'How does he feel about having partners?'

'I didn't tell him.'

'I feel uneasy about it. Lee's a good man.'

'I hate his guts. And to think that after all these years, I can finish him.'

'What do you mean?'

'That once we get that map, I'll kill him.'

'You didn't mention killing back in El Paso.'

'That was El Paso. This is Casa Grandes.'

'Johnny, I like Lee. I can't stand by and watch you murder him. Besides, there's no need for it. You said yourself there's enough gold for all of us.'

'It has nothing to do with the gold. I owe him. You'll keep out of it. You understand?'

'I can't let you do it, Johnny.'

Johnny's blue eyes slanted angrily. He grabbed her shoulders and sank his fingers and thumbs into her flesh. 'You don't know what that man did to me. Now keep out of my way or you'll get hurt.'

Twisting out of his grasp, she rubbed her shoulders. Pain darkened her pupils while her sensitive features turned blank and noncommittal. After a moment, she walked over and sat down on the bed. Her fingers still kneaded her shoulders, and her chin dipped as her gaze centred on a crack in the floor.

Johnny stamped to the window, stared down into the plaza. Dusk pooled along the edge of the streets, and someone lit a lamp in the *tienda* across the way. Two horsemen trotted in from the west. Off to the left, out of Johnny's line of sight, a dog yelped. A man in uniform stepped from the *alcalde's* office while a woman in a red dress sashayed over the plaza's north-east corner. 'Got any whiskey?'

'No.'

'Then I'll wash off some of this trail dust. We'll talk to our partner later.'

Lee tapped the dead ashes from his pipe,

75

slipped the pipe into his pocket. He should be angry with Aurora, but he understood Johnny Hughes's power over women because he'd seen Johnny at work before. That man could hypnotize a woman the way a rattlesnake hypnotized a rabbit. It was a talent that Johnny didn't mind using. He'd used and discarded a lot of women along the way, and Lee had a hunch that Aurora was next. He couldn't blame her; he could only pity her. Aurora probably worshipped Johnny, which meant she was in for a worse jolt than he'd experienced when he'd seen Johnny leaning against this bar.

Down to Lee's right a man chuckled and punched his companion on the arm. This fellow said something in Spanish; whereupon, the bartender joined in the rude laughter. Lee glanced around the room, abruptly aware that these men regarded him with open hostility. He stared down at the mahogany while his fore and middle fingers tapped softly against the wood. He didn't understand this resentment, but it must have been there all the time. His thoughts of Aurora and Johnny prevented his noticing.

Dropping a coin on the bar, Lee walked

outside. Dusk had fallen. Lamps flickered at the corners of the plaza while a breeze flowed along the street. So now, not only Ortega's outfit dogged his trail, but Johnny Hughes as well. He wondered how many other men in this country knew about him. His father had said that bringing that gold out wouldn't be easy, and, by God, he was right.

Two horsemen trotted in from the west while a uniformed man stepped from a corner building to stare after a woman in a red dress sashaying over the plaza. Across the street from where Lee stood, a church raised its adobe bell-tower skyward. The spicy odor of chile wafted from the café next to the cantina while two horsemen reined in to Lee's left. The woman in the red dress trucked into the hotel on the far side of the plaza. Next to the hotel, Lee saw a building with a *médico* sign painted on the window. The *médico's* office sided a building next to the stable that occupied the town's south-west corner, facing a street that led out of Casa Grandes toward the river and the distant mountains.

Lee's tongue touched the inside of his lip. He would gather his belongings and hightail it out of here. A half-moon shone above the sycamores bordering the river. He'd have enough light to travel most of the night, grab a few hours' sleep before dawn, then come morning, head for the mountains where he'd find hard ground to cover his tracks.

The hotel lobby was empty except for two men playing cards, and a clerk who scribbled something in his ledger. Crossing the room, Lee climbed the stairs, careful to step where the staircase met the wall so as to stifle creaking lumber. He followed the hall to room eight, paused to listen, and hearing nothing continued down the hall to his own room. As his hand closed around the door knob, he heard something thud against wood, heard the scuff of leather over flooring. Drawing the revolver from his waistband, he flung the door open on a surprised Johnny Hughes who whipped around from where he dug through Lee's saddle-bags.

Lee thrust the revolver back into his waistband. 'Looking for something?'

'As a matter of fact I am.'

'I figure you didn't find it.'

'Not yet, but I aim to.'

'Not in that pile of junk.'

'You're right. I've searched everything in

this room except you.'

'Then you'd better get back to your own diggings.'

'After I finish the job.'

'You've already finished it.'

'I want that map, Lee.'

'What map?'

'The one George gave you.'

'I don't know what you're talking about.'

'Sure you do.'

'We'll talk about it in the morning.'

'We'll talk about it now. Do you hand it over, or do I take it?'

'I don't think you can take it.'

Johnny's hand dipped to his side. His eyes sprang to triangular shapes as his lips formed a wolfish ring. 'You know damn good and well I can. Let's have it.'

Lee's mouth opened, closed. He could tell Johnny he'd burned the map after memorizing it, but his pride rankled at the thought. Still, he knew he was no match for Johnny with a handgun. 'Suppose you kill me and don't find it? What then?'

'You've got a point. Now do I take it or do you hand it over?'

Lee saw hatred in Johnny's eyes, the eagerness shaping his face. Johnny was two inches taller with a twenty pound weight advantage. Lee had seen Johnny fight, and Johnny had a brutal streak. But Lee couldn't utter the words that would resolve this. He'd resented Johnny's fake camaraderie back in El Paso, resented Johnny's using Aurora, and resented Johnny's confident assumption that he could just walk in and take over.

Johnny unbuckled his gunbelt, tossed it on to the bed. 'Don't you think it's foolish to take a thrashing?'

Lee's fingers curled around his revolver's butt. 'Since I'm the only one with any firepower, I won't have to.'

Johnny chuckled. 'You can't shoot an unarmed man. I can, but not you.'

The skin covering Lee's knuckles whitened. He understood Johnny's slur. It was a reference to the Yankee soldiers at Brandy Station. Lee flipped his gun on the bed, and as the six-shooter clanged against Johnny's handgun, Lee took two rapid, forward steps and slammed a fist into Johnny's chin. Johnny blinked, as he raised his hands, Lee's left flattened his nose, and Lee followed up with a right to Johnny's stomach plus a short, powerful hook to his kidney.

A glazed expression dulled Johnny's gaze,

and Lee felt exhilaration surge over him. He rammed ahead with fists flying, but in his excitement, he forgot to cover his advance. An uppercut sent pain streaking from his chin to the top of his skull. Bony knuckles smashed his lips, and warm blood, salted his tongue. He ducked an incoming right, drove a left into Johnny's heart, and deflected a hook that Johnny threw at his cheek. Lee ripped a jab into Johnny's ribs, caught Johnny with a slashing blow that opened a long, vertical cut at the corner of Johnny's eye.

Blood smeared Johnny's upper lip; blood drew a crimson line from his temple to his jaw, and his breath sawed in and out. Lee forgot caution. He hurled a looping right at Johnny's chin and closed for the kill. Somehow Johnny slid inside that overhanded right. He lowered his head and butted Lee in the forehead with a force that opened a three-inch, horizontal gash above Lee's eyebrows. Blood poured from that gash. It streamed down into Lee's eyes, blinding him.

Johnny was a blurred, wavering shape that slammed a fist into Lee's swollen eye. Pain exploded over his face as he buried himself in a shell of arms and fists and shoulders. Sharp, crunching hooks bounced off Lee's jaw, his temples, the side of his head. A jab stung Lee's ribs; a short uppercut rammed into his stomach below his protecting elbows, and a power-house hook crashed through his forearms and into his chest. Blood flooded Lee's vision. The blackened eye that Johnny had hammered felt puffed and full of grit. Lee's torn lips throbbed while the pain stabbing his battered frame left him sick to the stomach.

In the distance, Lee heard someone yelling, and that incoherent noise became words as Johnny pulled back from him. Lee heard Aurora's 'Stop it! Stop it! Are you both crazy?' and he swiped at his bloodied face until he could see her crimped features beyond Johnny's crimson visage.

Aurora poured water into a tin wash basin, wet a rag, and pressed that rag against the long gash on Lee's forehead. 'Hold it there,' she said, and wheeling back to the wash basin dipped a towel into the water, wrung it out, and cleaned the cut at Johnny's temple. Then she blotted the blood from Johnny's lips and threw the towel into the corner. 'I should have let you two kill each other.'

'I was doing all right,' Johnny bragged.

'I suppose you were doing all right too?'

Lee pressed the rag tightly against his pounding forehead. 'I've done better.'

'Why don't you two admit you need each other?'

'I don't need anybody,' Lee said.

Aurora snorted. 'Ortega's just waiting for you to reach that gold, and what about the Apaches? You need all the help you can get. Why be greedy? There's enough for all of us.'

'I still don't see where Johnny can help.'

'He knows the country, and he knows something about Indians. He'll earn his share.'

'And what can you offer?'

'I can keep you from killing each other.'

Johnny stepped to the bed, picked up his gunbelt, and buckled it around his waist. When his head came up, his eyes stared unblinkingly. 'You don't have a choice. We're in whether you like it or not. Now where's the map?'

Lee removed the rag from his forehead, felt blood ooze down his brow and pressed the rag to the gash again. He didn't know about Aurora, but he had an idea if Johnny could get his hands on that map there'd be two partners instead of three. Maybe he'd better let these people know just how important it was that nothing happened to him. 'I burned the map back in Fort Hancock. It's in my head.'

'Why didn't you say so instead of letting us beat the hell out of each other?'

'I didn't like the way you asked.'

Aurora looped her arm through Johnny's. Her full lips parted while her eyes glowed with satisfaction. 'Then let's leave it at that. Now you two shake hands and get some rest. I'm sure you want to head out come early morning.'

Johnny stuck out his hand and, as Lee gripped it reluctantly, Johnny said, 'Aurora's right. No reason we can't be friends. See you in the morning.'

Closing the door after them, Lee walked over to the tin basin where he washed out the rag and reapplied it to his forehead. He slugged over to the bed and lay down. He ached all over. With that blood blinding him, he hadn't been much of a match for Johnny. He was lucky Aurora had stopped it. It seemed he was stuck with them for now; but somewhere in the mountains, he had to lose them. Johnny's show of forgiveness might have fooled Aurora, but beneath that show lay a grudge that had lasted six years. Lee shut his eyes and wished the sick feeling in his stomach would go away. He knew what he had to do and he would do it.

6

At noon they reined into a U-shaped depression partially shaded by desert willow. Dismounting, Lee checked the mule's cinches and secured his animals. Johnny placed his hands over his kidneys and stretched, working the stiffness from his joints while Aurora used a bandanna to wipe the dust from her face. Lee rummaged through one of the packs and sorted out three tins of tomatoes, plus biscuits and fried ham.

Johnny crossed his arms at the wrists, interlocked his fingers, flexed. 'That's woman's work, Lee. Let Aurora handle it.'

Aurora walked over, picked up the supplies and found a flat rock to serve as a table. She made a fried ham sandwich and handed it to Johnny along with an 'airtight'. Turning, she placed two slices of ham between a biscuit and extended it in Lee's direction. He shook his head, said, 'I'll fix my own,' and stepped up to the makeshift table as Aurora punched holes into two airtights. When they had eaten, Aurora repacked the grub and stowed it in the pack.

Johnny rolled a cigarette. 'What a miserable way to live. I can hardly wait to shake the dust of this Godforsaken country out of my hair.'

Lee lit his pipe. He studied the toe of his boot and nodded reflectively. He recalled his surprise at finding Johnny in El Paso. Johnny's taste ran to fine wines, fine foods, expensive clothes, and refined surroundings, all of which were in short supply West of the Mississippi.

Surprise flushed Aurora's responsive face to be quickly smothered by the patient expression that hid her emotions. 'Do you plan to go home, Johnny?'

'South Carolina? No, I can never go back.'

Lee scratched the side of his neck. 'Money talks. Maybe those people could forgive and forget.'

'Maybe they could, but I can't. I'll never forget the day that pot-bellied carpetbagger strolled into the Point with that paid tax receipt in his hand. My whole life was wrapped up in that fat paw. It was too much for a gentleman to take, but you couldn't understand. You were never one of us. Your kind never owned anything, so you didn't lose anything. But not men like me. We'd had land. Money. Power. We'd been respected and feared, but the war reduced us to paupers. We had nothing left but our honor, and the Yankees and carpetbaggers wanted to take that. No, I can never forget or forgive, and I doubt that carpetbagger's friends would.'

One of the horses nickered as sunlight reflected off rock. Lee considered the toe of his boot again. He supposed Johnny was right. He didn't understand. But, then, he not only had owned little, he'd never felt the need for more. For him, this trip served a two-fold purpose. It would make life easier for his mother, plus satisfy his father's dying wish. Otherwise, for him, the gold changed nothing.

His gaze lifted to Aurora, whose attention focused on the distant mountains. He didn't understand how she fitted into Johnny's lifestyle. Johnny was a blue-blood who'd never made any pretensions concerning his feelings towards white trash or blacks. Of course Aurora wasn't black, but she wasn't a blue-blood either. Lee shook his head. He'd never imagined Johnny Hughes associating with a female who lacked *proper* credentials. He'd always thought too highly of himself.

Johnny flipped his cigarette butt into the brush. He stood up and pulling the Bull Durham from his vest-pocket, shaped another smoke. 'We're wasting time.'

As they stirruped on to their horses, Lee felt an odd, pressing sensation between his shoulder blades and swung to find Johnny eyeing him coldly. Then a smile tugged at Johnny's purpled lips as he threw a leg over the palomino and clucked him uptrail.

Lee brought up the rear. Tobacco sludge stung the insides of his busted mouth, and he spat out the sludge and stuck his pipe back in his teeth. That look in Johnny's eyes had mirrored his expression in Casa Grandes. Lee's gaze centered on the granite curves of the Sleeping Woman

Range. He couldn't beat Johnny with a gun, nor was he certain he could beat him with fists. A wise man would shoot Johnny in the back right now, but Lee had never been wise. The trouble was Johnny knew it. Johnny talked a lot about honor; however, talk about covered it.

The afternoon lazed by. Just as the desert had faded into mesa, the mesa faded into hills. Cedar and oak grew here. Yellowed grass covered the valleys, but that grass thinned as the hills reached the lower fringes of the Sierra Madres. The timber was replaced by scrub oak and mountain ash, and the land became a series of canyons and gullies.

When Johnny signalled a halt, the sun washed the forbidding landscape with its final glow. To their right, an inverted, V-shaped cave bore into the canyon wall. Johnny dropped from the palomino, said, 'Let me look this over,' and, leaving the palomino's reins trailing, hiked into the opening. In a moment he returned with a wide grin creasing his spoiled visage. 'That thing doglegs off to the left. We can build a fire in there with no fear of Apaches spotting it. Aurora, gather some wood and throw a meal together. I'm beat out.'

Aurora's shoulders sagged when Johnny disappeared into the cave. She stared at her hands as fatigue pinched her cheeks.

Lee dismounted. 'You take it easy. I'll get the firewood.'

Her shoulders straightened, and she gave him a quick smile. 'It's all right.'

He tapped the reins against his palm. Aurora's eyes had lost their lustre, and little tired lines fanned out from her lip corners. Trail dust clung to her shirt and trousers, and a sweat line darkened her sombrero. But fatigue could only dull the vitality that was so much a part of her, just as Johnny's thoughtlessness could only momentarily ruffle her feeling for him. Again Lee considered Aurora's place in Johnny's priorities and had an instinctive knowledge that it wasn't as high as Aurora believed.

He led his animals into the cave while Aurora unsaddled her mare. He noted that Johnny hadn't bothered to unsaddle the palomino and wondered if that was Aurora's chore. But Johnny had been raised to do nothing of a menial sort, and Lee supposed that a lifetime habit was difficult to break. Particularly if someone else was available for the job.

After hobbling the animals, Lee scouted the underbrush for firewood. A day in the saddle had stiffened his muscles, so any bending or stretching was painful. His left hand was still swollen, but the inside of his lips no longer hurt while his slitted eye, although tender, seemed less swollen.

Aurora placed a withered oak limb atop the armload of sticks she carried. 'This should be enough.'

Lee grunted and picked up one last piece of kindling. Black circles formed under Aurora's eyes; and her voice had trembled, but she gave Lee a ready smile as she turned back to the cave. He trailed her into the dogleg where Johnny, a cigarette dangling from his lips, sat with his back against the wall. The rank taste of anger filled Lee's mouth as he dropped his kindling wood where Aurora knelt and held a match to some splinters. Lee took out his pipe, tamped a half-bowl of tobacco into it. When Johnny glanced up, Lee turned so that Johnny couldn't see the contempt squaring his jaw. He couldn't let Johnny know that his lack of concern for Aurora was upsetting, for that would make matters worse.

After supper, Johnny lit another cigarette. 'We're deep in Apache territory. I think we ought to stand watch tonight.'

Aurora's hands squeezed together. 'Did you cut any sign?'

'No, but that means nothing. I'll take the first watch. Aurora, you stay on the lookout from ten to two when Lee will take over.'

Lee stared at the ground for a long moment. 'Aurora takes the first watch. That way she can get some uninterrupted rest.'

Johnny held his cigarette between his thumb and forefinger, puffed it slowly. 'You worry about finding that gold. I'll worry about Aurora.'

'She's worn out. Can't you see that?'

'We're all worn out. If you're so bothered, take both watches.'

Aurora sprang to her feet. She positioned herself between the two men. 'It's all right, Johnny. I'm too tired to stand watch now. Lee, maybe we should get some sleep.'

Lee nodded. He caught the anxiety in her voice, understood the worry that pocketed her cheeks. Aurora formed a tall, willowy shape but the fire's flickering light failed to hide her concern. Despite the fact that Aurora had used him, Lee had to admire her. She possessed a quality that Johnny Hughes would never recognize—a quality that money and background could never produce. Aurora was too good for Johnny and deserved better than he would give her.

A hand touching Lee's shoulder brought him instantly awake. He saw Aurora bending over him and beyond the orange fire, Johnny snored softly. Lee shoved the revolver into his waistband; he reached his feet as Aurora poured a cup of coffee from the smoke-blackened pot.

'You'll need a blanket.'

Lee grunted, clapped the blanket around his shoulders. She stood so close he could smell the perfume of her hair, and their gaze met when he accepted the cup of coffee.

Her voice was almost a whisper. 'I want to thank you for what you did today.'

He gulped the hot coffee to hide a sudden self-consciousness. To cover his confusion, he stooped for his rifle and, upon straightening, avoided looking at her. 'Get some rest.' He sidestepped her, paced around the dogleg, and walked to the mouth of the cave. Stars glittered overhead while the moon cast a pale light over the land. An owl hooted, and some faint fragrance sweetened the air.

Lee filled his pipe, turned back into the cave so that his body shielded the match's glow; then, he turned and stared into the night. The mule snorted, bringing a curse to Lee's lips. That sound would carry a long way. Inching into the open, Lee studied the smoky shadows. He saw nothing; heard nothing, and felt certain that the area was secure. Still, he wished that mule would be quiet. If nothing else, her snorting might wake Johnny and he didn't want Johnny awake.

Later, Lee pulled out his Waltham. The hands pointed at three a.m., and with mixed emotions, he studied the faded tintype; he'd forgiven his father, yet, he couldn't feel anything for a man he'd never known. He snapped the case and replaced the watch in his pocket. Why bother with regrets? The relationship with all its hurts and disappointments was finished. Perhaps he would never understand what, if anything, his father meant to him; but he'd elected to carry out the man's wishes, and he would do so.

He slipped back to the dogleg, saw that Johnny and Aurora were asleep. Then, he eased back to the cave's entrance, removed the hobbles from his animals and led them across the wash. Replacing the hobbles, Lee slipped back into the cave, tiptoed around the dogleg and, after picking up his saddle, returned to the entrance where he shouldered his equipment and hiked out to his hobbled animals. He strapped the pack on the mule, saddled the stallion, and after removing his hobbles, led the animals up the wash for about one hundred yards.

A rocky path fed off to the south, and Lee mounted the stallion after looping the mule's reins over the pommel. He had a good two hours of darkness before Johnny and Aurora awoke. Daybreak found him riding through rock-bound gullies that lifted toward higher land in the west. He saw the Sleeping Woman's outline off to his right and located a trail that flowed into a broad plateau spotted with yellow flowers. Reining in the stallion, he gobbled down the last of the ham, ate a can of peaches, drank from the canteen, and loaded his pipe. After stowing the empty peach tin in the pack, he wearily surveyed the foreground. The plateau consisted of flinty soil which suited his purpose, and he followed that gradually rising sweep of land until it ended in a series of gullies and draws with even rockier soil.

At noon he pushed out of the canyons into a broad sweep of white sand fronting craggy peaks that barred his westward progress. He hated to cross that sandy stretch but saw no alternative. The sun, a ball of fire, seemed to burn through his shirt, and he pulled the peak of his hat lower to shade his face. He felt sorry for the animals; this heat had to affect them, but he dared not water them since the crude map his father had sketched showed no water-holes between here and Sleeping Woman Ridge.

Some hours later the sandy wash gave way to a path that twisted through the mountain. Lee swung into that path gratefully. Johnny might follow him as far as the Sleeping Woman Range, but according to the map several trails branched out from there; and, at that point, Lee would lose him.

This path meandered on to another plateau leading towards jagged hill land. A sudden alarm rang in Lee's head, and he drew the stallion to a halt and dismounted. He squatted as his gaze followed the hoof prints breaking this gravelly soil. Those hoof prints were made by unshod horses, and when he ran his forefinger around the hoof marks' perimeter, he noted that the dirt had not yet caved in around the impressions formed by those down-driving hooves. These tracks were fresh, and his gaze searched the horizon as a worried frown puckered his brow.

He regained his feet where he thoughtfully thumbed tobacco into his pipe. As he passed a match over the bowl, it struck him that this country had changed him. He'd always been aware of weather patterns for his life had revolved around sun and rain. But now he found himself alert to other things—hoof marks in the sand, shifts in terrain, the subtle workings in a man's face. These were the things that mattered now; yet, he was surprised at how quickly he'd adjusted to these new demands.

Stirruping into the saddle, he realized that his immediate problem lay ahead, not behind. Johnny might or might not locate him, but he had to know not only who had left this sign, but how many riders were involved. He knew enough to assume that the people ahead were Apaches. It was also obvious that their trail pointed toward the Sleeping Woman Ridge. He had to locate them, then think of a way to evade them. During the two days he'd spent in El Paso, he'd learned that Apaches constantly slipped into the Sierra Madres to avoid capture by US troops. The Indians ahead were undoubtedly such a group.

The muffled plop of hooves rose over the plateau as Lee held the stallion to a slow walk. His gaze probed the horizon as he made his way toward the slope separating this plateau from the terrain beyond. Upon reaching that slope, the tart taste of danger coated his mouth, and his teeth clamped into the pipe stem. Some sixth-sense, made him pull rein again while he regarded the slope ahead. Feeling foolish, he slid from the horse, knocked out his pipe, and climbed the slope with stealthy determination.

Upon reaching the summit, he stared down into a narrow valley running between forested hillocks. In the center of that valley, eight Apaches squatted around a small fire. Lee settled his five feet, eleven inches into a depression, knowing that his only alternative was to wait the Indians out. Glancing down into the plateau, he searched for a place to hide his animals, but the plateau was barren except for the yellow flowers that flourished in the flatlands of this maze-like country.

Heat radiated from the rocky slope, and Lee's eyelids began to droop. The last three days had been hectic, and lack of sleep enervated him. He yawned, tried to squeeze the sleep from his eyes. His eyeballs burned from the gritty particles that seemed embedded there, and his eyelids were heavy flaps.

When his eyes opened, he knew from the position of the sun that it was late afternoon. His gaze jerked into the valley below, and he saw nothing but open land. He'd been lucky, for those Apaches could be roasting him over a fire if they'd ridden this way. He took out his watch, realized he'd slept for three hours. That knowledge jarred him because it meant that Johnny couldn't be too far behind. He had to move now!

7

Dawn's cool greyness welcomed Lee. As he rolled to a sitting position the thud of horse hooves beat into camp. Apprehension jerked Lee's head around as Johnny Hughes and Aurora trotted into view.

Johnny laughed as he pulled rein. He thrust his thumbs into his vest pockets as his wicked gaze studied Lee from across the distance. 'I figured you to make better time.'

'Would have, but I ran into Apaches.'

'One man's loss is another man's gain. Aurora, get out that pot and boil some coffee. Might as well have some of those tortillas, too.' The grin widened Johnny's lower face as he shaped a cigarette, held a match to it. 'Lee, it sure is good to be with somebody from back home. Somebody you can trust.'

Lee set his plate aside, picked up his coffee. Their arrival had killed his appetite. Damn those Apaches anyway. His gaze followed Aurora's trim form as she walked to the river where she dipped a coffee pot into the water. Gaze on the toes of Johnny's boots, he punched tobacco into his pipe with a silent 'God damn!' He held a match to the pipe and his head lifted to find Johnny's scornful gaze taunting him. Johnny stood with his thumbs in the pockets of his fancy vest, his planter's hat pushed back to reveal thick, blond hair. Lee shook out the match, dropped it as his gaze shifted again to Aurora. It struck him that she seemed perfectly at ease here, but then she'd seemed perfectly at ease back at Fort Hancock. Lee had the notion she'd be at ease anywhere.

Johnny flipped his cigarette butt into the fire. 'That coffee's ready, Aurora. Break out those tortillas and let's eat.'

Handing Johnny a tortilla, Aurora poured a cup of coffee and sat it next to where he squatted on both heels. She glanced at Lee. 'You still hungry?' and at his head shake, filled her cup and munched at a tortilla.

'How much farther, Lee?' Johnny asked.

'About a day's ride.'

'Good. I'm sick of this. I'm ready for a bath, some good food, and a bottle of ten-year-old bourbon.'

A trickle of smoke escaped Lee's lips.

He was sick of this too but for a different reason. He knew Johnny too well to expect an amicable arrangement when they reached their destination. Despite his show of goodwill, Johnny hadn't forgotten Brandy Station, and even if that old dispute didn't lie between them, he was too greedy to share that Canyon de Oro loot. It would come to a showdown, and Lee despised his inability to take Johnny off guard. But murder wasn't in him. Never had been.

Fifteen minutes later, the three of them swung into their saddles. On their side of the river, the land stretched hard and flat while beyond the river high cliffs loomed. This mesa was covered with sagebrush and rabbit brush while yellow flowers mushroomed in circular bunches. Far ahead the mesas rammed into a mountain range, and the river disappeared behind a wall of rock.

Near noon they reached the mountains bisecting the plateau. The river flowed through a channel of solid rock that dipped slowly towards sea level, and the trail breasting the river edged to slippery shale bordered by towering slabs of granite that would shut off the sun as it moved westward. The green-blue water hissed around polished boulders as its turgid flow turned into rapids that flung spray toward the shoreline.

After a meal of tortillas and tinned peaches, they continued on foot because the trail was so slippery they feared the horses might fall and hurl their riders on to the rocks. Lee led the way, with Aurora following and Johnny holding the rear. The sun shifted in its westward course, and shadows blued their journey. The only sounds in this walled outlet were the click of hooves against stone, the swish of leather across shale, and the slap of water breaking against rocks.

Aurora's scream echoing up those granite walls wheeled Lee sharply around. He saw Aurora's right foot shoot out from under her, watched her claw empty air as she pitched headlong into the rocks. That scream frightened Aurora's mare. Her front hooves lashed open space while her eyes flared in their sockets, and Lee held his breath when those flailing hooves connected with the slippery shale.

Letting his horse's reins trail, Lee scooted back to where Aurora crumpled on the rocks. Johnny slithered in from the rear, and anger shortened his lips. He reached

Aurora at almost the same moment Lee did and waited, with his thumbs hooked in his vest pockets, while Lee turned Aurora over. Her lips were the only color in her drawn face. Her mouth sagged open while her eyeballs rolled back under her lids. Her legs twitched when Lee grasped her belt buckle, and as he worked her body up and down, pink spots pulsed slowly into her cheeks.

Lee helped her to a sitting position, glanced at Johnny. 'Had the wind knocked out of her. Let's hope that's the worst of it.'

Johnny snorted, pulled out his Bull Durham. 'Leave it to a woman to pull a stunt like this.'

Lee knelt down on one knee. He placed both hands on Aurora's upper arms while he examined the knot on her forehead. 'You all right now?'

She nodded as a slight smile tugged at her lips. 'I think so.' She gripped Lee's elbows, and when he pulled her erect pain stitched her cheeks. 'My ankle. The left one.'

'Sit down. We'll take a look.'

A disgusted grunt exploded from Johnny's lips. 'Jesus Christ, Aurora, can't you do anything right!'

Lee's teeth clicked together. He started to say something, then busied himself removing Aurora's boot. His fingers probed her leg, and she moaned when he flexed her ankle back and forth. 'Could be worse. There's no bones broken.'

'Then what's the problem?' Johnny snapped.

'Probably a sprain.'

Johnny flung his cigarette at his feet. 'Well, don't look at me. I'm no doctor. Aurora, do you think you can walk?'

'I can try.'

Lee's fingers pressed along her ankle again. 'No chance of that. This thing's already swelling.'

Johnny's teeth shone between parted lips. He kicked at a loose rock. 'I knew we should have left her in Casa Grandes. On the trail, a woman's nothing but trouble.'

The river danced on its noisy course. The shadows darkened in this rock-lined V, and the shrill cry of a hawk rang throughout the canyon. Lee thumbed tobacco into his pipe, but his attention stayed on Aurora. He saw the hurt in her eyes, a hurt that physical pain hadn't put there. 'Aurora will have to ride the mule. She's the sure-footedest creature we've got. Walking's out. Maybe if

Aurora takes care of that ankle, the swelling will go down by tomorrow.'

Aurora's arm closed around Lee's shoulders as he drew her to her feet. Her brown eyes were inches from him, and once again he noticed her curious, womanly smell. That fragrance caught in his throat, and he glanced quickly uptrail when she balanced against him as she hopped along on her good ankle. When they reached the mule, he slid one arm under her knees and lifted her on to the pack astride the mule's back.

'All right. Let's hump it,' Johnny grumbled.

Lee bit his lower lip. Johnny had just lit another cigarette, and he flipped the match into the river before he wheeled and climbed back to his palomino. Lee's hand closed around his pipe as his gaze followed Johnny's retreating form. He was getting a bellyful of Johnny's blatant concern for number one. Lee stuck his pipe back in his mouth, heeled around. Aurora's slim, erect back centered his line of sight bringing a recollection of the moment he'd lifted her on to the mule. He'd never suspected her willowy shape was so womanly. As he manoeuvered cautiously back to his horse, he shook his head. If Aurora thought Johnny was unconcerned now, wait until they reached El Paso with that gold.

When they reached the end of the shale, they found themselves on a bench which ran along the base of great cliffs. The ground was flat, stony, and empty of vegetation, and Lee found himself comparing this barren place with the sloping hills, the rich soil, the towering pines of his native South Carolina. Back home the countryside was dotted with cattle while squirrels, rabbits, and foxes roamed the forest. Here only lizards, snakes, and, perhaps, gila monsters flourished.

They crossed this bench, rode through shaded canyons to reach another plateau. The river dropped a hundred feet here following the curves it had drilled through solid rock, and they found themselves looking down at that silvery sweep instead of breasting it. The plateau abruptly terminated at a sheer drop; whereupon, Lee and Johnny worked their mounts across this cliff until they found a trail sloping down to the land below.

After traversing that tortuous descent, they reached firm-soiled bottom land.

The river flowed sluggishly again, a late afternoon sun reflecting off its surface. Lee packed his pipe and fired up as they rode over a stretch of weed-covered flats separating them from the river. Lee felt more at home here. The river's gurgle was like music while along its shallow banks Mexican piñon, willow, and sycamore provided welcome relief from the monotony of the treeless country behind.

An hour's ride brought them to the edge of another cliff where the river pitched downward in a green-white waterfall. Spray drifted around them, and Lee swung away from the drop to a circuitous trail that led to a shallow pool at the base of the waterfall's seventy-five foot plunge. By now the sun formed a red ball on the horizon while dusk cooled the land. 'We'll camp here,' Lee said.

Johnny removed the planter's hat, ran a hand over his thick, blond hair. 'Good idea. It's a fairly open spot with plenty of water.' He stepped from his palomino, brushed the dust from his frock coat and black, broadcloth trousers. 'Good God! What I wouldn't give for a drink.'

Lee ambled back to the mule. He

considered Aurora's pinched face. 'How's the ankle?'

She smiled, glanced at Johnny before her brown gaze settled on Lee. 'It should be better by morning.'

'I'll help you down.'

Johnny jabbed his shoulder into Lee's back and pushed him aside. 'I'll take care of her. You take care of your business.'

Lee shrugged and walked back to his stallion where he fumbled with the cinch buckle.

'Lee, leave these animals saddled. I don't expect company, but if we get any we'll have to ride.'

Lee's hand released the cinch buckle, and he stared toward the darkening horizon. That advice made sense; yet, he resented the insolence in Johnny's voice. Lee led his animals to the river where he watched them drink. He'd learned a lot during his few days on the trail, but he had more to learn. Apaches hadn't crossed his mind. After the animals had drank their fill, he tied them to a sycamore. 'Guess we could risk a fire?'

Johnny looked up from where he had settled Aurora on a blanket. His gaze searched the distance as he shaped a cigarette. 'I think so.'

Lee pulled the coffee pot from the pack and after gathering some twigs and several dead branches built a low fire.

Footsteps squished through sand as Johnny strolled over. 'I thought you said we'd reach that gold tonight.'

'Looks like I was wrong.'

Johnny half-turned, hooked his thumbs in his vest pockets while his distrustful gaze settled on Lee. Johnny's lantern jaw bunched as hostility carved hollows in his quarrelsome visage. 'I've about had it with you. Don't try another stunt like the one last night. I won't stand for it.'

'No worry. I couldn't lose you if I wanted to.'

'You were a fool to burn that map. Sometimes I wonder if you know *where* you're going.'

'I know. Now dig out some tortillas and let's eat.'

When Lee came awake, pink and gold streaked the sky while a mockingbird's whistle shrilled from the sycamores. Johnny still sprawled on his blanket, but Aurora

110

limped up from the river, coffee pot in hand.

A second mockingbird whistled from down river, and morning's cool smell mingled with the crushed fragrance of sycamore leaves. Lee yanked on his boots, reached his feet, and tramped to the river where he splashed water over his face. He turned to find Johnny sitting on his blanket, a cigarette dangling from his lips. An angry, impatience roughened Johnny's cheeks, but Lee ignored it, paced back to his blankets, and strapped them behind his saddle.

Boiling water hissed as Aurora dumped a handful of coffee into the pot. Lee checked the pack's lashings, adjusted its contents, bent down to give each animal's hoof a thorough inspection. When he had completed his chores, Aurora called, 'Breakfast.'

After eating they killed the fire, scattered the ashes, and boarded their horses. When Lee directed his stallion into the river, Johnny's 'What's going on here?' sounded short and strident to the rear, but Lee urged his mount into the river. The water rose to Lee's knees, and he had to kick the recalcitrant animal into the waterfall.

Green and white water pressed against Lee's head and shoulders, momentarily blinding him; then, his horse cleared the waterfall and stepped into a cave's dark recesses.

Horse hooves drummed softly as Johnny and Aurora rode into view. It was so dark in the cave that Lee couldn't see the expression on their faces, but he didn't have to see Johnny's face to know his thoughts. Lee quickly dropped from the saddle and, putting the stallion between him and Johnny, sidestepped back to the mule where he pulled three pitchpines from the pack. 'Johnny, get down. We need some light in here.' When Johnny stirruped from the palomino, Lee swung around the mule and thrust a pitchpine forward. As he'd expected, Johnny's right hand closed around the pitchpine and Lee held a match to it.

Lee lit another torch and handed it to Aurora; then, he lit the third one and held it overhead. The cave was nine or ten feet high and about fifteen feet wide with a narrow tunnel arcing back into the mountain, and Lee watched closely while Johnny stalked around the circumference.

'I don't see a damn thing,' Johnny said.

'That tunnel bears off to the right. The gold's back there.'

Pitchpine in his left hand, Lee watched Johnny's gaze dart toward the tunnel. His teeth showed in a wide grin as he swaggered over to Aurora. 'I told you I'd make a rich woman out of you.'

Aurora didn't return that grin. She glanced from Johnny to Lee while a cautious expression straightened her lips. Then she looked at the ground as a blank composure shut off her thoughts.

Johnny gave her a long, puzzled look, then grinned at Lee. 'What are we waiting for?'

Lee heard the excitement in Johnny's voice, knew he should share that excitement, but it didn't come. Instead of the violence Lee'd expected the moment they reached this place, he'd encountered an outgoing grin. He didn't like playing games, and he'd just as soon Johnny forced this. No matter how it ended, Lee preferred it over and done. He considered Aurora's closed expression. Her cheeks were brown satin that revealed nothing, but all her placidity couldn't hide the fear and uncertainty pulsing behind her controlled features.

113

Johnny hiked over to his palomino. 'Come on, Lee. Let's get on with it.'

Lee moistened his upper lip with his bottom one. He felt perspiration dampen his chest, his shoulders while a stale, tinny mixture coated his tongue. He couldn't outdraw Johnny, but maybe if he pitched forward on his belly as Johnny's pistol cleared leather, that first shot would go high. 'I know how you feel, Johnny. You've hated my guts since Brandy Station. I say we finish it here and now.'

Knitted lines crisscrossed Johnny's forehead. He chuckled as he shook his head. 'Lee, that was years ago. You don't know how good it is to see somebody from back home. Somebody you can trust. This is no time to bring up the past. Let's load up and get back to civilization.'

Lee kept his gun hand near his revolver. He didn't buy Johnny's talk. He hadn't been too friendly back at Casa Grandes, so why the act now? Lee knew he had to push this because otherwise he'd never be able to close his eyes until he reached Fort Hancock—if he reached Fort Hancock.

Aurora glanced in Lee's direction, relief stamped on her face. 'Johnny's right. We have to move. Don't forget that Manuel

Ortega's behind us.'

Lee nodded. So that was it. Johnny needed him which meant he didn't have to worry until Johnny needed him no longer. 'I'll lead the way.'

Their footsteps echoed throughout the cavern as they hiked up the tunnel. Moisture had settled here, and the smell of rank earth permeated this place. The tunnel twisted right, then left before emptying into a second room almost twice as large as the one behind the falls. The torches spread light over this vault, throwing light on a pile of canvas bags stacked along the far wall.

'There it is! By God, there it is!' Johnny whooped. He rushed over the cavern and dropped on his knees by the canvas bags where he tore open one of the sacks and dug out two handfuls of nuggets. Johnny dropped the nuggets back into the sack and dug out two more gleaming handfuls. 'I'm rich! Rich! I can have it all again. No, better. A big house. Servants. The finest horses. It'll be just as it was before the war.'

Lee paused by the stallion, torch held high in his left hand. Excitement finally hammered in his chest while a huge grin drove across his face. They'd made it! They'd really made it! If only his father were bending over those sacks instead of Johnny, but no need to think of that. From the corner of one eye, he glanced at Aurora. Apprehension, not delight, drew her lips downward, and he glanced back to the front not understanding it.

As Lee advanced toward the far wall, the odor of rotting canvas reached him; then, he stared down at the stacks of canvas bags, fresh excitement tightening his throat. What filled those bags changed everything. His mother would never scrub another shirt, wash another greasy pot, mop another floor. And the farm. He could afford the best stock. The best of everything. Aurora stood at his elbow. Her passive appearance revealed nothing, but he sensed her withdrawal, the emotional fence that enclosed her. Abruptly, he realized that Johnny's future hadn't included Aurora. That Johnny had ranted about 'I' not 'We'.

'Let's get to work,' Lee said.

Johnny rubbed his hands together; he laughed and greed kindled a glow in his eyes. 'You load the packs while I hand the stuff to you.'

8

After the mules were loaded Johnny lit a cigarette. He inhaled deeply and expelled a streamer of smoke. He gave Lee a long, thoughtful look; then, he walked over, picked up the gunbelt and buckled it around his waist. Afterwards, he located Lee's pistol, stuck it in his waistband, and handed Aurora her gunbelt. 'I don't think we'll be needing you any more, Lee.'

Aurora gulped air as a startled expression drove the color from her face. Her eyes sprang into wide circles, and she stared at Johnny in disbelief.

Lee felt a brassy taste creep up his throat while his stomach seemed to collapse on itself. He'd stood here like a damn fool while Johnny'd got the drop on him. All along Johnny had planned to take him out as soon as the gold was loaded.

Aurora's hand went to her throat. 'Johnny, we've still got to reach Casa Grandes. Manuel Ortega is out there, and what about the Apaches?'

'We can head north and cross the border at Agua Prieta. Manuel Ortega won't bother us.'

'But that's Apache country. I'd rather face Ortega.'

Smoke curled from Lee's pipe. He stared at his revolver settled in Johnny's waistband. 'Apaches are out there. I told you I'd run into a party. Otherwise, you'd never have overtaken me.'

Johnny chuckled. 'Don't make much difference why we caught up. It's going to end the same way.'

Aurora took three short steps that put her directly between Lee and Johnny. 'Please, Johnny. Haven't we had enough killing?'

'I told you how I felt back in Casa Grandes. Now move or I'll have to move you. I mean it Aurora. I don't want to hurt you, but I've waited a long time for this.'

Aurora stiffened as her hands closed at her sides. She was two inches shorter than Lee, and he could see Johnny's unyielding visage three feet beyond her right shoulder. In the pitchpines' flickering light, Johnny's shadow threw a threatening shape on the wall behind him, and that wavering light threw other misshapen shadows over the cavern's damp, moldy interior. Lee abruptly realized that his own shadow spilled forward. With Aurora directly between them, Johnny couldn't be exactly sure of Lee's position or the distance separating them.

Johnny removed the cigarette from his lips, dropped it to the ground. 'Do as I tell you, woman. I'm not playing games.'

Lee slid his left foot a few inches forward as Aurora murmured something he didn't understand. All his faculties were focused on Johnny's grim-lipped visage, and he dragged his right foot a few inches forward, saw no change in Johnny's expression, and inched his left foot forward again. He repeated the process as spasms ripped over his lower back. He'd advanced about a foot without Johnny's noticing. If he could cover the distance to Aurora, he had a chance. She'd buckled her gunbelt around her waist, and the gun's black butt gleamed invitingly. Lee understood that Aurora and Johnny were finished because she hadn't been included in those New Orleans plans; but he had to believe she still meant enough to Johnny that he wouldn't kill her. Once he got an arm around her waist, she'd form a human shield. Then both he *and* Johnny would hold a pistol, making negotiations a possibility.

A bit jangled as one of the horses shook its head. Darkness coiled around the cave's perimeter while the tunnel's opening formed a dim outline off to the right. Lee's feet slithered forward inch by inch, and he saw indecision pocket Johnny's cheeks. Then the toe of Lee's boot struck a rock protruding from the cavern's floor, and that dull thud sounded like a thunderclap in the hushed silence.

With a yell, Johnny sprang forward, and his left hand batted Aurora to one side. His gun hand rose and, as Lee threw his arms up for protection, the gun barrel crashed alongside his head and hurled him into a red-streaked oblivion.

Voices sounded, but those voices made no sense. Red circles swirled in a black void, and Lee seemed to swim up as that blackness shaded to a light grey. Something pounded the top of his skull, but it was a muffled pounding that came from inside not out. As that sound gained in intensity, pain rammed through Lee's body in a steady rhythm.

He heard voices again while something

damp and cool brushed his forehead, his cheeks, his lips. The grey area blocking his sight grew lighter; images solidified beyond that light, and Aurora's concerned features hung before him. Her head and shoulders came into view, and when the coolness touched his forehead again, he realized that she sponged his face with a damp cloth. He tried to sit up, but his eyesight blurred. His arms lacked the strength to steady him; the top of the cave whirled, and he fell flat on his back.

'He'll be all right,' Aurora said.

'Not for long he won't. I mean to kill him. Didn't you see what he was trying to do? If he'd got hold of your gun, we'd both be dead.'

'I can't believe that.'

'Believe what you want, but you've got to make a choice between him and me. My advice is to start thinking about yourself.'

'Is that what you're doing?'

'Exactly.'

'And what about me?'

'This had nothing to do with you. I owe him from way back.' Johnny grabbed Lee's shirtfront, hauled him to a sitting position. 'You can quit faking it. I didn't hit you that hard.'

Pain slammed through Lee's head as he sagged in Johnny's grip. The surroundings refused to stay still, and Johnny's grim countenance shimmered in broken waves of light. When Johnny released him, Lee put his palms flat against the dirt floor to steady himself. His vision cleared; but his head still throbbed, and he felt sick to the stomach. Gorge soured his throat as Johnny stepped back from him, and the metallic click of a six-gun's depressed hammer sounded far away.

'If you kill him, you'll have to kill me too,' Aurora said.

Johnny threw her a disgruntled look. 'Get those horses and mules out of here. I don't want a gunshot to startle them.'

'I mean it, Johnny. The minute we run into Mexican authorities, I'll tell them about this. If we don't meet anyone, I'll tell the marshal at El Paso.'

'You'd turn on me?'

'I swear I will.'

Lee tried to bring things into focus as Johnny's teeth bared. He stared at Aurora for a long moment, then released the hammer and slammed the revolver into its holster. 'All right, we'll do it your way. But we take the horses and the mules.'

Aurora seemed to wilt as warmth seeped into her face. Her palms opened in a relieved gesture, and she stepped forward to lay a hand on Johnny's arm. 'You won't regret this.'

'I already regret it.'

'What about Lee? How does he get back to Casa Grandes?'

'He walks.'

'But it's several days on horseback. What does he do for water?'

'I'll leave him a couple of canteens. Now let's ride.'

Aurora's throat worked as she searched for words, but she shut off whatever she wanted to say. She threw Lee a final glance, eyelids closed down so that he could not see the thoughts behind those dark lashes. Then she whirled for the horses.

'Wait for me in the other cave. I'll be along in a minute,' Johnny said. When she hesitated, he glared at her. 'I said we'd do this your way.'

After Aurora gathered up the reins, Johnny flicked Bull Durham into a paper as she led the animals into the tunnel. He thrust the tobacco sack in his pocket, rolled the quirly with one hand, stuck it in his lips, and lit it as Lee pushed to one knee and crawled to the rear of the cavern where he sat with his back against the wall. Johnny's hatred pulsed across the distance, and Lee wondered how a man could hate so much for so long. But Johnny's code said that even a suspected wrong, if not righted, was a reflection on a man's honor. Johnny had corrupted that code, for there could be no honor in deliberate murder.

Johnny's lips formed a cruel ring. 'If you get back, I'll be in New Orleans. I don't figure you've got the guts, but if you have your part of this loot will be there for the taking. Maybe Aurora was right. There's better ways to handle this than shooting you. That would be too easy.'

When Johnny heeled toward the tunnel, Lee said, 'What about the canteens?'

'They'll be by the falls,' Johnny answered as he disappeared behind a rocky turn.

Johnny's retreating footsteps was the only sound in the high-ceilinged vault. The rank odor of damp earth left a moldy taste in Lee's mouth while the pounding between his ears dimmed to a slow cadence. Gently he drew his fingertips across the side of his head. A ridge raised from his temple to the back of his skull.

When he looked at his fingertips, he found no blood, but a dull ache pulsed behind his eyes, and he fought double vision.

Lee pulled at the skin on his neck as a dryness scratched his throat. He wished Johnny had left those canteens here. He was too weak to fetch them. At least the queasiness had left his stomach, and only a dull ache stabbed his skull. He thought of Aurora as he fished his pipe from his pocket, sucked at the empty stem. Lee's fingers dug into the dirt near his thigh as he tried to steady his vision. He wondered if Johnny meant to share that gold with anyone. Aurora had earned her share.

He looked at his father's watch. A quarter to eleven. They'd spent the morning in this cavern. Suddenly he felt trapped, for these walls began to close in on him. He needed fresh air, needed the sun's warmth on his back, needed to wash this foul taste from his mouth. His gaze lingered on the faded tintype before he closed the watch cover. If, *no, when,* he reached the border, he'd find Johnny Hughes. His father spent fifteen lonely years looking for this cache. Lee wasn't about to let those years add up to nothing.

The ridge alongside Lee's head hurt, and

sweat beaded his face. He stood up and, carrying one of the pitchpines for light, staggered into the tunnel. He felt beat out. He'd just about recovered from the fight in Casa Grandes, but Johnny had put him back in a hole with that pistol whipping. The noise of the falls rustled just beyond the next turn, and the air smelled fresher here. His pitchpine cast shadows over the elongated cave while the rustle of the falls became a loud murmur. He spotted the two canteens plus a revolver and gunbelt off to the left, hiked over, slipped the canteens' straps over his shoulder, and buckled the gunbelt around his waist. The canteens were empty, but only four feet separated him from the falls and fresh water.

The outside air offered a welcome relief to the cave's dark interior. The sun, now directly overhead, burned the chill from Lee's body, and he shucked off his boots and gunbelt and waded into the pool's green depths. That water slaked his thirst, refreshed his spirit, soothed the dull ache behind his eyes.

Later, he sat on the grassy bank and waited for the sun to dry his clothing. Casa Grandes was a long walk. He would make it only if he conserved his strength. Johnny and Aurora were already two hours ahead, and although their top speed would be a fast walk, he had no chance of overtaking them. Somewhere along the way he would find two dead mules, for those animals were overloaded. They could never hold up in this heat unless Johnny dumped part of their load, and he was too greedy for that. He would drive those mules until they dropped, then, out of necessity, take what gold the horses could carry.

His clothing still slightly damp, Lee slipped on his boots, picked up the canteens plus his gunbelt. His head pounded again, but he had to move. Perhaps, after he left the river, he would travel at night to hold down his fluid intake; but until he reached the trail breaking away from the river, it would be easier to travel by day.

Kneeling down, he dipped the canteens into the water. When they were full, he stood up and slung them over his left shoulder. As he swung toward the pathway squiggling up toward the mesa, his left leg felt wet, and he glanced down to see water dripping from the canteens. The water had soaked through his trousers, and, when he turned the canteens upside down, he found two holes punched in their bottoms.

With a curse, he hurled the canteens against the rocky embankment. There was no way a man could cross the country ahead without water, and the tortillas tucked inside his shirt were a cruel joke. Without water, those tortillas would drive a man crazy with thirst.

He pulled his hatbrim over his eyes and climbed the trail that led to the mesa. He had no choice but to attempt the return journey. He might last several weeks if he remained in the mountains with its plentiful water, for game had to live somewhere in these rocky draws. Once his ammunition was gone, he'd starve here as surely as in the plateau and mesa country. Everyone called this Apache territory, so gunfire would undoubtedly bring them down on him. Better to die in an effort to reach Casa Grandes than to roast over an Apache fire. Besides, his stubborn nature demanded that he go out fighting rather than sit here and wait for death.

Upon topping the rise, he pinpointed six Apaches about a thousand yards out from his position. They rode westward in single file, and he flattened behind a butte until they disappeared into the mountains.

Then he followed the river, staying in the shade of the willows and sycamores as he hoofed toward higher ground. By late afternoon, he approached a slope that rose to higher land and locating the trail he and Johnny had found the day before, hiked up its rock-bound entrance. The heat, the dust, and the walking had turned the dull ache behind his eyes into an agony that increased with every step. Otherwise, except for lack of breath, he felt fine. He had trudged behind a mule for too many years for walking to affect him. His legs were the strongest part of his body, but he knew that once he gained the top of this slope he must stop for the night. This headache was a killer, and he could only pray that sleep would cure it.

9

When Aurora slid from her mare, fatigue traced little tired lines down her slim cheeks, formed dark half-circles under her eyes. Dusk shaded the land while shadows crept out from the boulders sheltering the knife-like arroyo Johnny had selected for their camp.

'Aurora, fix something to eat while I check these mules. No fire tonight. We can't be too careful.'

She watched Johnny stride back to the mules, then pulled a sack of tortillas and airtights from her saddle-bags. For the hundredth time that day her thoughts shot back to Lee, but she shoved those thoughts aside and dropped wearily to the ground. At first, when Johnny had told her about the gold and how they would share it, she'd been elated, for she'd dreamed of the things wealth made possible. But she hadn't known Lee then, and she hadn't known about the animosity between Lee and Johnny. She wanted the gold but not enough to murder for it. Although she'd agreed to trick Lee as a means of getting in on the treasure, she'd hated leaving him without a horse. Despite what Johnny said, it was murder.

A hot breeze stirred through the arroyo. A flock of nighthawks winged overhead, and a coyote's lonely yodel lifted from the distance. Aurora glanced at Johnny who checked the packs and cinch belts, a cigarette dangling from his lips. She

130

wondered if he knew how strong that tobacco odor was. If she could smell it, an Apache could catch the scent for half a mile. It didn't make much sense to worry about a fire when Johnny smoked one cigarette after another.

Johnny clumped back to her and squatted off to one side. He removed his planter's hat, flicked perspiration from his hair, set the hat on the ground, uncorked the canteen, wet his handkerchief, and wiped his face. He seemed relaxed and good-humored as his gaze raked the surroundings. 'Three more days and we'll be across the border. I told you a person could do worse than stick with old Johnny.'

She handed him a tortilla plus two cans of tomatoes and pulled a second tortilla from the bag as he punched holes into the cans with his pocket knife. After he handed her one of the tomato tins, she munched unenthusiastically on a tortilla. She was sick of tortillas, sick of tomatoes, sick of dust, sick of the whole affair. Worst of all, she was sick at heart. She'd never claimed to be an angel, but what she'd helped do to Lee had sunk her to a new low. He was possibly the only decent man

131

she'd ever met and, at the thought of him, the tortilla tasted like a mouthful of sand. Johnny had smashed that gun barrel against Lee's head so hard she couldn't believe it when his eyes had opened. She'd thought the blow had crushed his skull.

She washed the last of the tortilla down with the tepid tomato juice. Johnny had finished his meal, and his fingers shaped a cigarette. He hadn't appeared to notice her weariness and seemed trapped in thought while his fingers worked automatically at the quirly. For some reason she remembered how Lee had helped her gather wood while Johnny had rested, how Lee had shown concern for her sprained ankle while Johnny had griped about the delay. Then her gaze touched Johnny; and she tried to feel guilty, but the guilt refused to come.

It was so dark that Johnny's square-shouldered form was no more than a blot in the heavy dusk. But Aurora didn't need light to remember every facet of his handsome face. That handsomeness had drawn her to him in the beginning, that plus his quick smile and ready laugh. They'd had good years together, years she'd thought would continue although

Johnny had never mentioned marriage. But this trip had changed Johnny. Some of his statements had upset her, and much of his time was spent in the withdrawn, secretive mood that separated them now. That mood, along with other attitudes he'd revealed the past few days, frightened her because it told her that Johnny possessed character traits she'd either overlooked or never noticed. She sat there a long time wondering about the stranger who slumped across from her. Then the moon's pale circle rose over the enclosing rocks, washing the area to a melted-butter yellow.

One of the horses nickered, bringing Johnny out of his reverie. 'We'll have to stand watch tonight.'

Aurora strained to read his thoughts. She couldn't dispel her feeling of apprehension, and her fears urged her to ask questions she sensed were better unasked. 'What happens when we reach the border, Johnny?'

'This is no time to think of that. We've got all sorts of problems ahead of us.'

'I need to know, Johnny. I can't explain it, but I feel something's changed.'

'Nothing's changed.'

'Then we'll go to New Orleans together?'

A match flared in his cupped hands as he

lit a cigarette. The odor of tobacco struck her, and she sensed a tightening around his lips. To hide its red glow, he kept his hands cupped over the cigarette while his head dropped to shadow his face. 'I'm not from this part of the world, Aurora. As you well know, I've never liked this country, and only the war, plus certain other circumstances, brought me here. I don't fit in, Aurora. I never have. You wouldn't fit in where I'm going. You wouldn't like it.'

'I thought after three years we...'

'I never promised you anything.'

'No, you never did, but I thought...' She shut down on the words as understanding numbed her. She'd never realized how much she'd depended on Johnny, how big a space he'd filled in her life. She looked down at her hands, squeezed them together in a futile gesture. 'I could learn to fit in.'

'Aurora, you don't understand. It's not something you learn overnight.'

She looked down at her hands again. This shouldn't hit her so hard. She'd known since the moment Johnny had let those nuggets cascade through his fingers he'd changed. But admitting it had been too difficult; shoving it into the back of her mind had been easier. Perhaps the worst of it was knowing Johnny had never considered her an equal. Other men had looked down on her; and certainly the so-called 'good' women had labeled her a tramp, but Johnny had always treated her with consideration. It hurt to realize he'd played a game. Tears formed in her eyes, but she blinked them back. She had never cried and she wouldn't cry now; still, she couldn't stop the tears that fell into her heart.

Johnny lit another cigarette, again cupping the match's flare in his hands. 'Look, I know you're upset, but there's no need for it. You'll get your share of what's on those mules. You can do anything you want. You'll never have to worry about money again.'

'I guess money doesn't mean as much to me as it does to you. I keep thinking of the good times we had together.'

'You're just like Lee. You never had anything, so you don't know what it means to lose something. Aurora, I was born a gentleman. Until the war I never did a lick of physical labor in my life. A Nigger laid out my clothes, another Nigger served my meals, and still another one saddled my horse. People said, "Mister Hughes" when I walked by, and Hughes Point was the finest estate in South Carolina.' Johnny stood up and hurled the cigarette against a rock. As ashes sprayed out, he stared off toward the top of the ravine. 'The last three years may have been good for you, but I've loathed every second. Wearing these clothes, playing for two-bit stakes, associating with roughnecks, drinking swill instead of whiskey, being held in contempt by men and women not fit to clean my boots, and then to have to walk back to a miserable little adobe shack that lacked even the slightest degree of good taste or comfort. Not any more, Aurora. Those packs are my way back to where I ought to be, and I'll step on anyone who interferes.'

The ache in her breast was almost unbearable, and she had the odd sensation that she hovered somewhere off to the left watching this. It was as if it were happening to someone else, or as if she had somehow split into two people.

Johnny sank down on a rock, leaned forward with his forearms resting on his thighs. 'Don't take it so hard. Like I said, you're well fixed. This is the beginning, not the end.'

Words stuck in her throat, and she kept fumbling with the buttons on her shirt. It was almost impossible to believe that she'd lived with this man for three years, shared every intimacy and every thought without having the faintest insight into who or what he was. Men had been a big part of her existence since she was eighteen years old; she would have staked her life on the fact that no man could have fooled her so completely. But this one had, and here she sat unable to cope with it.

'Why don't you get some rest,' Johnny said. 'I'll wake you later. From now on, we've got to keep our eyes open.'

'I can't rest now.'

'Then you take the first watch. Frankly I'm beat.'

She watched him walk to the palomino, unstrap his blankets, throw them out on the ground, and lie down. She felt drained and everything seemed to move in slow motion. Johnny lay with his back to her, but she didn't need to see his face to visualize his every feature. She'd always considered him an open, unselfish individual, so it shocked her to discover his real values revolved solely around himself. For her part, she'd always been above-board in their relationship and had made no secret of her love and loyalty. Reflecting back, she knew she'd seen what she'd wanted to see, blinding herself deliberately to Johnny's faults.

An owl hooted somewhere in the aspen forest. The breeze had cooled, but they were not high enough for it to be unpleasant. The knowledge that she would be alone again, that there would be no one with whom she could share the trivia of her days compacted the loneliness of this desolate spot. Suddenly she wanted to scream, to yell, to jump astride her mare and ride wildly and thoughtlessly across the night; but this was Apache country and despite her need for some kind of relief, she dared not move about. For just an instant her mind rebelled, said 'To hell with it'; then, the tough, resourceful core that had sustained her through so many disappointments shoved that defeatist attitude aside. Yes, she loved Johnny and would find it difficult, perhaps almost impossible, to live without him, but live she would.

As morning's first light filtered into the arroyo, Johnny walked over to Aurora and nudged her awake with the toe of his boot. He heeled around before she could say anything, stalked back to the animals where he pretended to examine their hooves. He didn't want any more of last night's discussion, and the best way to avoid it was to hit the trail. After a moment, he glanced over to see Aurora roll up her blanket and hike across the gully to the mare. While she fastened the blanket behind her saddle, he lit a cigarette and drew a whiff of smoke into his lungs, waiting for her to say something. Instead, she unpacked foodstuffs from her saddlebags, walked over to him, and handed him a tortilla and a can of peaches.

After they'd eaten, he mounted his palomino and led the way north. Her lack of concern had relieved him at first because he couldn't afford woman problems right now; at the same time, it hurt his vanity. He'd always believed he'd held Aurora in the palm of his hand, but it was obvious that her outpouring of affection had contained about as much substance as his. Well, what should he have expected! He'd met her working in some crummy saloon, pushing drinks and fleecing drunks. Her job had been to sell the illusion of love, but he'd needed a woman, and, at that particular time, he'd never imagined he'd one day resume his former lifestyle. So he'd sold her a bill of goods and taken up with her; only, now it appeared she'd sold him the bill of goods. Aurora had been extremely useful since nothing distracted a man more than a lovely woman's coy flirtations. He'd turned a lot of cards because of Aurora's slim legs and full bosom. Still, he considered himself a woman's man, and it irked him to know that this tart had played with him.

Up ahead the mesa fed into sheer cliffs where a shale trail paralleled the river. They'd walked that trail coming in, but he intended to ride out. The horses were more sure-footed than Aurora, and he didn't need another stupid accident. She'd been lucky she hadn't broken her ankle, and it was undoubtedly still weak which would make it more difficult for her to navigate that slippery path again. He should have left her in Casa Grandes because, on the trail, a woman became just one more problem.

He glanced over his shoulder and caught

a glimpse of her stolid features. He'd be glad to reach the border where he'd be rid of her. The mules seemed to be holding up fine, but their heavy load slowed their progress. Actually, they were overloaded, and he had to take care that those mules reached the border. Then they could drop dead as far as he was concerned.

They passed through the shale-filled valley to ride onto a broad plateau reaching toward the Sleeping Woman's lower heights. Johnny grinned remembering the surprise lengthening Lee's farmer's-face when he and Aurora had ridden up two days ago. It reminded him of the disbelief in Lee's eyes when he'd discovered his part of this trip had terminated.

Later they rode by the charred remains of a fire to climb into rougher terrain, where the land was a jumble of draws and culverts winding through short stretches of woodland and meadows only to swing back into more rock-bound pathways.

Somewhere nearby a horse nickered, and Johnny heard the click of shod hooves on rock soil. The trail bottlenecked into brush and timber, and out of that bottleneck trotted Manuel Ortega accompanied by three riders. Across the distance, Johnny saw Ortega grin. More hooves clicked to the rear, jerking Johnny's head around to where three more horsemen closed in from the gully shooting off to the right.

Johnny's throat went dry; that same dryness puckered his mouth and, although it was hot here in the open meadowland, he felt a chill. He threw Aurora a quick glance, noted her shortened lips were the only sign of emotion in her forced composure. Then his gaze flicked ahead as he reined in the palomino.

The banditos halted a horse's-head from Johnny's palomino. Ortega's huge grin stayed fixed on his politic countenance revealing wide, tobacco-stained teeth. One hand swept off his sombrero, He made a mock bow, then clapped the sombrero back on his thick mop of sweaty black hair. 'We meet again, *señora,* but where is my good friend, your husband?'

Aurora managed a smile. 'He'll be along shortly.'

Ortega laughed. He scratched his bulging belly. He tapped the quirt in his right hand against his thigh; his gaze went beyond Johnny to the mules. Greed shone in his suety cheeks, and his smiling visage failed to hide the baser impulses of his character.

'I see you have acquired another mule. Paco, see what is in those packs.'

The squat Paco dismounted, and when he reached Johnny threw him a deadly stare. Johnny forced himself to hold that stare, but the slight, upward curve of Paco's lips told the story. He sensed Johnny's fear; they all sensed it, and it made the moment more enjoyable. Johnny considered the two men flanking Ortega. One was a slender fellow with a purple scar reaching from the corner of his left eye to the bony thrust of his jaw. Like Ortega, this man wore a big hat, bandoleers, and two pistols hung from his belt. A bold, avaricious expression stained his cheeks, and he picked his long nose with his little finger. The second individual bulked large in the saddle. He was short and flabby with pig eyes and a brutish expression that made Johnny's flesh crawl.

A yelp lifted from the rear, followed by Paco's, 'Gold, Manuel! More gold than I thought was possible!'

Ortega's meaty lips opened, closed, and he drew a hand across his heavy jaw. The thin bandit chuckled as his forefinger traced the ugly scar while the flabby fellow's brown eyes glittered as he dug at his front teeth with a dirty fingernail. Johnny half-turned in the saddle, so he could see the other men closing off the rear. One was a youngster with boyish features, but there was nothing boyish about his smirk. His companion, a thick-set, grizzled old-timer, stroked a flowing, grey mustache while an uninterested expression shut off any show of excitement at Paco's discovery.

Ortega's grin widened. He rubbed his hands together. 'Raul, let's take a look. Gordo, watch this one.'

With that, Ortega and the tall Mexican on his left dismounted and swaggered past Johnny toward the mules. When they hustled by Johnny's palomino, Ortega slapped its flank while his *'Bueno. Bueno,'* grated against Johnny's ears.

Johnny glanced at Gordo whose eyes had closed to baleful slits. Otherwise, Gordo sat loose and flaccid in the saddle, but Johnny caught the expectation behind that blank visage. Gordo wanted him to make a break. They all did.

As Johnny swung round so that he could observe Ortega and Raul, his gaze found Aurora. She sat quite still; her head tipped forward, and she seemed to be studying her hands. Her complexion had paled, her jaw-line had ridged, but otherwise she maintained her composure. Johnny's attention swung back to Ortega and Raul. They had reached the mules where Ortega dug his fingers into the pack and pulled out a handful of nuggets. He looked at Raul; whereupon both men laughed as Ortega dropped the nuggets back into the pack. They walked around the mule where Ortega examined the contents of the other pack. They laughed again, slapped each other on the shoulders.

The young fellow to Ortega's rear nodded, and even the older man's meaty lips parted in a smile. Ortega pulled at one ear, stared at the ground while Paco adjusted the pack straps. Raul's knife-sharp visage pointed in Johnny's direction. All these men were silent, watchful, waiting for Ortega to voice his thoughts.

Ortega's head came up. He popped his pant's leg with his quirt. Flashing another grin, he stalked back to Johnny where he paused with his hand on his pistol butt. 'It seems you have done well.'

Johnny tried to smile. Fear was a stone in his gut, a constriction in his oesophagus. 'Don't get any ideas. Right about now, Lee Keene's lying on that last rise aiming a rifle at your backbone.'

Laughter bubbled from Ortega's throat as he slapped his left hand with the quiet. 'He's lying back in those hills sure enough. Right where you shot him before you took his gold and his woman.' Ortega's gaze shifted to Aurora then and lust formed pockets in his suety cheeks. 'I have thought of you often, *señora*. Beauty like yours stays with a man.'

The tapping of Ortega's quirt beat over the area as Johnny's strained countenance swung to Aurora. She held her position, refusing to look in Ortega's direction, but a resigned awareness drove the last trace of color from her complexion. Johnny's gaze flicked back to Ortega, and he read the hunger in that feral face as Ortega's eyes stripped Aurora's clothing, garment by garment, from her willowy shape. Raul's thin silhouette moved within an arm's reach of Johnny's palomino, and Raul's expression mirrored Ortega's animal needs. Paco remained by the mules while the two outlaws behind him stood in fixed anticipation. The older man still seemed unconcerned, perhaps bored, with the situation, but the boyish one's beardless cheeks flamed with passion. He'd forgotten

Johnny and the gold. He saw only the woman.

Johnny's pulse quickened. His gaze darted over the arroyo as thoughts streaked through his brain, but Gordo's cunning expression jerked Johnny back to reality. Helplessness flooded him, and he understood complete despair. Aurora played a different hand. She could satisfy certain needs, and she had enough experience to keep those needs alive. He, however, could offer this bunch nothing except the gold which they would take anyway. He remembered the revolver at his hip. Ortega hadn't bothered to disarm them because he thought no one would be crazy enough to pull a gun. Since a dead man had nothing to lose, Ortega had thought wrong.

Ortega smiled. 'Gordo, take this one back in the canyons and show him the way north. But first we must have his gunbelt.'

A rank taste seeped into Johnny's mouth. Spasms ripped his belly. 'If you think there's a lot of gold in those packs, you haven't seen anything. There's three times that much back in the mountains, and I can take you to it.' He felt his heart flutter wildly at the way Ortega's eyelids narrowed, and he knew he'd found a weakness. He held his breath when Ortega glanced at Raul, but the scar-faced henchman's malevolent expression didn't change. Johnny squared around so that he could bring the three men near the mules into his line of vision. They'd heard, and their greed was as strong as the smell of cordite after a gunfight.

A crow's *caw* rasped from the aspen-covered slopes beyond the arroyo. One of the horses shifted its weight and leather squeaked. Ortega's bear-like form tilted backward and forward while his left hand toyed with the quirt's long tassels. Then his brutal features pointed at Johnny, and his smile became a grin. 'I like what you say. It is better for men to be partners than to quarrel over what cannot be changed. At first, I thought to send you on your way since I had found you with my good friend's wife and suspected the worst. But even she claims he is back in the hills, so I, perhaps, misjudged you. Take us to the gold.'

Raul cleared his throat, spat out a ball of phlegm. 'Why waste time with him when the woman can take us?'

'Don't count on Aurora. She has no

sense of direction,' Johnny said.

Ortega chuckled softly as his hungry eyes devoured Aurora. 'Is that true, *señora?*'

Aurora's big eyes stared at Johnny; her head dipped affirmatively as Ortega chuckled again. 'It seems we have no choice.'

Ortega's cheeks plumped out with reflection as he studied each of his followers. 'Leon, you will remain with the mules. On our return, we will take them to camp and fetch fresh animals.'

While Ortega walked back to his horse, Johnny rolled a much needed cigarette. Ortega's patience wouldn't last long. This day and, perhaps, another. If a break came, it would have to come soon.

10

Early morning found Lee stumbling along the shale-bottomed path where Aurora had sprained her ankle. Even at this hour, the sun's reflection off the shale's surface created a smoky heat that caused Lee's head to throb. Johnny's gun barrel had landed solidly yesterday, and Lee wondered if he had a slight concussion. The throbbing had subsided during the night; yet, he'd felt light-headed and at times his vision had blurred. Also, that nauseated feeling had stayed with him, and that, plus the empty stomach twenty-four hours without food had produced, left him weak-kneed and trembling.

His boot slipped off a rock, and he pawed the air in order to maintain his balance. That near fall sent shock waves through him, and the sycamores at the mouth of this V looked fuzzy. He sank to his knees, waiting for the pain to ease while he caught his breath. This lack of energy upset him, for he was in good shape. But he'd suffered several physical as well as mental poundings the last few days, so the effect, perhaps, was catching up with him.

By five o'clock, he'd reached a camping area. His best bet was to leave the plateau and seek shelter in the enclaves of rock and brush that fed into the canyon country. To his left the slope of the Sleeping Woman Range shot upward in a series of granite cliffs dotted with aspen and firs until it reached the Woman's six thousand feet ridge. To his right, the plateau sloped toward another distant mountain range, while ahead lay a country of innumerable gullies and draws and brush-lined arroyos.

He advanced through the pass and clipped through the surrounding cliffs. This pass emptied into a wash that led through another break into the higher country beyond. He decided this wash offered the kind of campsite he wanted, but, before settling in, it seemed a good idea to climb the mole-colored boulders facing him for a look at the land ahead; then, once he'd assured himself that nothing moved out there, he could rest his aching feet and throbbing head.

A series of scooped-out depressions formed an almost perfect stairway to the top of the boulders from where he had an unobstructed view of the canyon. He ducked instinctively as his gaze located a group of horsemen about a thousand yards out trotting straight toward him, but he stood up when he realized this group was not Apaches. For a moment, he rebelled against what his brain told him; then, he admitted Ortega's broad-brimmed sombrero topped the head of one of the lead riders, and his breath caught when he recognized the two individuals behind Ortega and his companion. Aurora and Johnny had walked right into it, so their only reason for being alive had to be their willingness to lead Ortega to the caverns behind the falls.

Abruptly, Lee realized he stood in plain sight and quickly dropped behind the boulders. Three other banditos rode behind Aurora and Johnny, effectively boxing them in, and Lee scratched at his stubble of beard, wondering how to handle this.

He had to decide upon some plan of action, and fast because the horsemen were already close enough for him to recognize Raul who flanked Ortega while Paco, Jaime, and Leon brought up the rear. The flabby Gordo was missing, but he could have remained in camp, or Johnny could have killed him. Lee's anxious gaze swept the area. If they reached the plateau, he could do nothing. Too much open ground. He had to trap them in this wash. As he drew his revolver, the party reached the narrows that dipped into this shallow bowl of land—close enough for him to see the strain on Aurora's face, the satisfaction layering Ortega's fleshy visage.

He waited until they loped into the center of the bowl before firing his first shot. The revolver sounded like a bomb blast that sent Ortega and his men digging for their sidearms. The frightened horses reared on hind hooves, and Aurora almost slipped from the saddle when her animal snorted and pitched sideways. Ortega shouted, 'Take cover! Take cover!' whereupon, the whole group darted to a line of broken rocks and pulled in behind their protective surface. Even as the revolver bucked in his hand, Lee slipped from his perch to dash toward an overhang off to his left. The ring of scrub oak and boulders walling off the wash hid him completely until he found another angle that looked down on the line of rock'sheltering the bandits. A head lifted above that rock, and Lee fired again, then legged it farther around this egg-shaped circle. He fired from a third position, moved and fired again, then triggered two more rounds as he approached the dip through which Ortega's party had just entered.

At that instant, the shocked Mexicans sent a volley of lead arching over the draw. Knowing they fired at shadows, Lee grinned as he punched fresh shells into his handgun. He'd intended to kill Ortega with the first shot, but the bullet had gone high. The fact that Ortega's men stayed behind that ledge told Lee they hadn't figured this out. If they'd known they faced a lone tenderfoot, they'd have scattered over this wash and hunted him down. He had to keep moving, firing. Maybe they'd think other bandits surrounded them, or, better yet, that Apaches held this higher ground.

He slammed five quick rounds into the rocks where Ortega gathered and scurried across the incline separating him from the south side of the wash. By now his breath came hard, and his head ached terribly. After punching more cartridges into his revolver, he climbed a scrub-oak-covered ridge that gave him a perfect view of the opening that led into Ortega's retreat. He couldn't see anyone because they huddled back under the overhang, but satisfaction puckered his lips since from this point no one could leave that hideaway without giving him a clear shot. Bad luck had placed Ortega in a hole, and Lee intended to keep him there until he figured a way to reach Aurora and Johnny.

As the afternoon light faded, shadows

crept over the wash. Lee stretched full length on the ledge, his attention fixed on the passage to Ortega's hiding-place. The shadows thickened as the sound of leather scraping against stone lifted from directly below Lee's position. A man's head and shoulders edged into view, and when this man moved into the open, he formed a solid spot in the dusty gloom. Lee wasn't sure whether he lined in on Paco or Jaime, but when the revolver's blast reverberated off the basin's rock walls, the man screamed as he pitched forward.

The next time he looked at the watch it was 3 a.m. The moon was far to the west now, the shadows deeper. He crawled to the end of the ledge where he climbed down on an oak-studded slope that led to the wash. When he paused for breath, he heard the scuff of footsteps and pulled behind a scrub oak just before two men edged into view. He recognized Paco's heavy black beard, and the other fellow's boyish figure could only belong to Jaime. From here, he could drop them both, but any shooting would warn Ortega, and he didn't want that.

Paco and Jaime halted opposite the scrub oak. Lee could faintly hear sibilant whispering, but they spoke in Spanish. Paco pointed off to the left, and, as Jaime scurried back down the wash so that he followed the shadows to the far side, Paco eased off in a direction that would bring him to the south pass.

Climbing down from the ledge had worsened Lee's headache. His stomach heaved and, for a moment, he fought the urge to throw up. He held his place until Paco faded into the rocky outline ahead; then, he slipped down the trail Jaime had followed, for it fronted the opening that led into the rocky recess where Ortega held Aurora and Johnny. When Lee reached that shallow draw, he dropped to his belly and peered around the granite abutment. The dead man's light-shirted form still sprawled in the funnel-tipped passageway, and Lee's gaze followed that funnel as it widened into the oblong shelter where Ortega waited. He saw Ortega and another man hunkered down by a small fire near the right wall. Both men drank coffee. They seemed completely at ease although they kept a bored attention on the narrow-lipped passageway.

Twelve to fifteen yards ahead, the horses, reins trailing, were penned in a rope corral.

Aurora and Johnny were not in sight, but the two men by the fire kept glancing at a spot beyond the animals. The quarter moon had reached a spot so that its glow left a velvet blanket swirling along the side of the funnel where the horses were penned. If Lee could reach those horses undetected, they would form a buffer zone between him and the men by the fire. That fire was no more than glowing coals, so the far side of the hide-out should be fairly dark. He had to reach Aurora and Johnny, free them, and some way he couldn't figure, ride out of here. Any shooting would be instinctive because light was too poor for good aim. He needed another pistol since Johnny was the better shot and the two guns would even things. The dead man's revolver lay in its holster, but Lee couldn't reach it. Then he remembered Johnny had a knife.

Creeping around the abutment, Lee wormed through the velvet blanket that flowed into the shadowy recess. He moved slowly, fingering the trail ahead for protruding rocks that might bruise a rib, or worse, a rotting bush that might pop under a down-driving knee or boot. All this concentration and arduous physical activity had turned his headache into arrow-points chipping his skull. The nausea had returned, and he felt light-headed.

Ortega's gaze swung in Lee's direction, and cold sweat popped from his pores. He knew Ortega couldn't possibly see him; yet, Ortega's primitive instincts were so strong that Lee knew a moment of panic. Abruptly, his thoughts shot back eight years to another night when he'd snaked through a fog much like this one toward a Yankee outpost. He'd sweated then as he sweated now, and he hadn't been able to shake the notion that those Yankees could see him despite the darkness.

When Ortega's gaze slanted back to the fire, Lee elbowed forward. The acrid smell of dust pricked his nostrils; sweat layered his body, and he had to fight the nausea pushing up from his stomach. He reached the horses, where he slumped against the ground waiting for the animals to become accustomed to his scent and presence. If they started shuffling around, Ortega or his companion might investigate. Lee drew his revolver. Should either man start for the horses, he would let that man get close enough for a certain shot, then try to down the other bandit. But he didn't want it that

158

way. He might miss the second shot and all hell would follow.

The horses sensed him. They threw wall-eyed glances in his direction and craned their necks, but his stillness silenced their fears. Lee let out a breath he didn't know he was holding and bellied around the rope corral to a point where he had a clear view of the place. As he'd suspected, the fire's glow failed to light the area, leaving plenty of darkness for maneuverability. Aurora and Johnny sat six-seven feet from him, but they were no more than grey blobs in the darkness.

As he crept forward, Lee watched the two men by the fire. When he crawled an arm's length from Aurora, her gaze found him and a startled gasp tore from her lips. That gasp brought Ortega to his feet. His wide-chested form lined in Aurora's direction while alarm dimpled his cheeks. The other man kept his seat, but one hand dropped to his revolver's butt while his surly face turned grim and attentive.

Lee's thumb rested on his pistol hammer. If Ortega stepped this way, he was a dead man. Dryness constricted Lee's throat. Aurora stiffened in an unnatural position, but Johnny's bored. 'How long do we have

159

to sit here before you untie us?' reassured Ortega who grunted contemptuously before resuming his seat.

One of the horses nickered. Ortega's companion dumped a handful of coffee into the pot sitting on the coals, and a strong coffee odor permeated the dugout. Lee shoved the revolver in its holster, armed across the remaining two feet and squirmed behind Ortega's prisoners. He ran his palm along Johnny's back, felt the knife, and removing it from its sheath cut the rope binding Johnny's hands and feet. After freeing Aurora, Lee put his lips close to Johnny's ear. 'I'll take Ortega. You get the other one with your knife.'

'It's too dark and he's too far away. Give me your gun.'

Lee hesitated, glanced at the men by the fire. He didn't want to give Johnny the revolver because if they pulled this off, it gave Johnny control.

'Give me the gun. I'm the better shot and you know it. As soon as I fire the first round, you and Aurora go for the horses. Grab three reins, cut the rope, and stampede the rest.'

Lee reluctantly thrust the pistol into Johnny's hand. He didn't like it, but they had to get out of here before those two men prowling the brush returned; then, he'd contend with Johnny.

'Move!' Johnny's yell was drowned out by the handgun's magnified roar recoiling off the low-ceilinged dugout. Lee grabbed Aurora's hand, pulled her to her feet, and sprang for the makeshift corral. Two revolver blasts echoed simultaneously, and lead screamed off rock. Lee grabbed the rope, said, 'Aurora, pick up those reins,' whereupon, Aurora dropped to her knees, and grappled wildly. One forward and backward slash of the knife parted the rope corral, and more shots sounded as the ends fell free.

The horses neighed. They stamped around in place until Lee realized that, despite their fear, those trailing reins held them. He picked up one end of the slashed corral rope, and used it as a whip to drive the terrified animals forward where more shots plus Lee's yells and the stinging rope lashes forced them into a trot despite their training. A gunshot exploded next to Lee's ear, and Johnny rushed past to grab his palomino's reins from Aurora and leap into the saddle. Screaming at the animals clogging their passageway, Johnny spurred ahead while Aurora and Lee sprang onto their mounts and thundered after him. Lead zipped past Lee's head; Ortega's cursing rose over the bedlam, and then they cleared the funnel's narrow opening to wheel across the wash. Dust boiled up. Four more shots shattered the night. Up ahead Johnny rode low on the palomino's neck while Aurora's slender shape formed an outline in the quarter-moonlight.

Lee yelled, 'Get down, Aurora! Get down!' and abruptly found himself flying through the air. As his head and shoulders jammed into the dirt, pain slammed through his body in one giant hammer stroke. When he rolled to his back, he saw his horse crumpled ten feet to the rear and vaguely remembered gunfire when they'd galloped through the cut. Red blurred his vision as he tried to push to his feet. The surroundings seemed to quiver like the ground under his feet. Several more shots boomed over the depression, and an orange steak flared from atop a boulder off to his left. A low, drumming noise beat against his skull, swinging his unfocused gaze up into Aurora's pale features as she reined in beside him.

From a distance he heard Aurora's, 'Get

162

up behind me,' and somehow he stuck a boot into an empty stirrup and, with her hands tugging at his shoulders, hauled himself up behind her. Pistol shots ripped the air. Lead sang off rock. As Aurora wheeled the horse, Lee locked his hands around her waist. His world spun. Bile clogged his throat, and he closed his eyes and rested his head on Aurora's shoulder.

He was sick. Sick! His arms had lost their strength, and he felt his grip loosening. He heard hoofbeats. Thunderclaps. He opened his eyes to a quaking horizon while the bile pushed up from his throat to sour his mouth. Cool air fanned his face, and he gulped that air as he fought the nausea rising from his stomach. The ground flashed beneath him. He was slipping. Slipping. But from some deep reservoir, he found the energy to clamp his fingers in a saving vice.

Time ceased to exist. He only knew the wind cooled him; his hands formed a buckle around Aurora's waist, and his head throbbed in time with the down-driving horse hooves.

Later he gazed up into the star-studded night where his blurred vision found two dim shapes looming directly above him.

His fingernails scratched through dirt. A rock stabbed his left shoulder while a terrible pain tightened around his skull. He didn't remember getting here, didn't remember falling from the horse, didn't remember anything but pain, pain, pain...

A match flared, followed by the stale odor of tobacco. The match left a dying, yellow streak across the night as Johnny said, 'We've got an hour or two before they catch their horses. Those animals won't go far with their reins trailing, but it gives us time to reach Gordo and that gold.'

The universe spun again. Lee heard Aurora's, 'Don't talk like a fool. How long do you think we can stay ahead of Ortega with those mules?'

The tip of Johnny's cigarette glowed, followed by a long silence; then, the cigarette glowed again. 'You're right. Our best bet is to head for Casa Grandes. Get more mules and backtrack to that cavern.'

'I don't know if Lee can ride.'

'Look, I'm not wasting time on Lee Keene.'

'I'm staying with Lee.'

Johnny's cigarette glowed briefly before it drew a yellow-orange streak in the dark.

'You're a fool, Aurora, but that's your problem.'

Johnny bent down and, unbuckling Lee's gunbelt, pulled it from beneath him. Then, when Johnny moved back, leather squeaked, and Johnny's head and shoulders silhouetted the horizon as horse hooves rang against rocky earth.

11

After Johnny had cantered off, Aurora considered her situation. She was abruptly aware of the shadows creeping out from nearby hills, an owl's thin hoot, the rustle of scattered scrub oak, and none of those things were reassuring. For years she'd depended on Johnny, and she felt frightened and alone. Then she gritted her teeth and sat down by Lee. She'd survived before Johnny, so could she now.

She put a hand on Lee's cheek. It was cold and clammy. She felt the collar of his shirt, ran her hand down inside his shirt front. Lee was soaked with cold perspiration. She touched his cheek again and fought down the helplessness that flooded her. She removed his hat, so that she could see his face, but in the diffused light she couldn't tell if his eyes were open or closed. She stood up, walked over to the mare, brought the canteen back to him, and dampening her neckerchief wiped his face. She said, 'Lee, can you hear me?' and when he faintly nodded, her relief was so great that she had to fight back the impulse to laugh.

Recorking the canteen, she stared off into the distance. Although Lee was conscious, he was too weak to be of any help which meant she had to make some decisions. They couldn't just sit here because Ortega would soon be along. Should they ride double and head for Casa Grandes? Would they be able to stay ahead of Ortega! She pressed her palm to her mouth, tried to think coherently. She had to get control of herself because that all important element, time, couldn't be wasted on doubts, fears, and self-pity. But she didn't know what to do! She was no doctor. To move Lee might kill him.

Suppose she were in Ortega's boots! He'd be considering the gold. He'd know there was an outside chance that Johnny and Lee could not only overcome Gordo but, with luck, reach Casa Grandes. Ortega wouldn't be concerned with his former prisoners. Sure, he'd wanted her. His brutal gaze had raped her every five seconds, but the gold was the key.

That realization steadied her. If she could get Lee into the hills, find a spot to hole up, they would be safe. She had the tortillas plus two canteens of water. She'd hide out, let Lee rest for a day or two before heading for Casa Grandes. The only possible concern was water, but she could ration that.

She walked back to the mare and placed the canteen's strap over the pommel, then swung back to Lee where she dropped to both knees. 'Lee, you're going to have to help me. I'm not strong enough to put you on that horse alone.'

A shrill yelp sent shivers racing down her spine, and her head jerked in fearful anticipation, but it was only a coyote. She was falling apart which was stupid. They were in no danger, so she had to forget her fears and make things happen. She squatted behind Lee, slid her hands under his armpits and lifted, but he was dead weight. She yanked with all her strength and brought him to a sitting position. Then she stood up, bent down, and grabbing him around the waist tried to heave him to his feet. When he failed to budge, she yanked again, but she couldn't move him. Just this little effort left her short-winded. Her arms trembled while the bitter taste of defeat coated her mouth. 'Damn it! Get up!' she whispered savagely in his ear. His body tensed, and, when she heaved again, he pushed awkwardly to his knees. Her breath ran out in one long flow as she braced herself against his back and, with his help, hauled him to his feet.

Aurora balanced Lee against the mare, put both his hands on the pommel, and, keeping her right shoulder positioned against his lower back, shoved his left boot into a stirrup. Then she placed both shoulders under his buttocks, and, muscles straining, helped him crawl aboard the mare. Her forearm rested on the mare's back, and she rested her head there. Thank God Lee wasn't a big man, or she would never have gotten him astride that horse.

The moon had long since slipped behind the western peaks. Soon dawn would creep in from the east. She glanced at Lee who sagged loosely in the saddle. His head and shoulders slumped forward so that shadows hid his face, but she noticed his hands gripped the pommel tightly. Despite his dazed condition, he understood the necessity of sticking to that saddle. He had to stick because she didn't believe she could muscle him aboard the mare again.

After a moment, Aurora picked up the reins and led the mare toward the hills. She didn't know how to cover her trail but figured it didn't matter. Ortega's thoughts were elsewhere, and she didn't think anyone could hide a trail from an Apache.

Daylight found her hoofing through a wide-lipped canyon. She stopped near a stunted oak where she dropped wearily to the ground. It had been over twenty-four hours since she'd slept, and her energy quotient equalled zero. They were far from Ortega's path now. It was time to settle in. Her gaze found Lee's shallow visage. If she was beat out, he had to be beyond exhaustion.

Half-way up a sloping hillside, she spotted a break partially covered by a cercocarpus's drooping branches, and pushing to her feet she trudged up that slope until she reached the break that channeled into a six by eight enclosure with rock walls and an open ceiling. If she tied the mare at the rear of this space, she would be unable to see into the canyon, and this would prevent the animal from nickering or neighing should other horses come into view. Aurora liked the feel of the place and, deciding she could find no better, urged the mare around the outcrop and secured her to one of the cercocarpus's arm-sized branches.

She took Lee's arm, shook him until his pupils appeared between slitted lids. 'Just hang on to that pommel and slide down. I'll help you.' Grasping his belt, she leaned her one hundred and ten pounds into him as he slid from the saddle. Bracing his arm across her shoulders, she supported him as they wobbled into deep shade where he sprawled out across the ground despite her attempt to lower him gently.

With great effort she pulled him to a sitting position, and, after retrieving a canteen and the bag of tortillas from the saddle-bags, held the canteen to his lips. When she broke a tortilla into bite-sized portions and fed him, he ate slowly, methodically, his glazed eyes closing once he'd given the area an uninterested glance. Even that slight awareness brought a sigh of relief from Aurora's clenched lips. All Lee needed was rest. Suddenly, she wasn't so tired any more. They'd make it. She knew they'd make it.

After he swallowed the last of the tortilla, she held the canteen to his lips again, recorked it, and making a pillow out of a blanket, helped him lie back under the cercocarpus. For her, rest was out of the question. She had to watch the canyon. Not that she could do anything, but she'd feel more secure if she kept her eyes open. By now sunshine yellowed the land, and she found a niche that provided a view of the canyon.

She washed a tortilla down with water and, after giving the mare a drink, made herself comfortable as she prepared to wait out the day.

A collared lizard reared up three feet out from where she sat and scurried on hind legs into a crack between two small boulders. A hawk floated high in the distance, and a climbing utas rustled the leaves of the overhanging cercocarpus. Aurora broke off a leaf, chewed the stem while images of the past flipped through her

171

memory. Strangely enough, she no longer felt bitter at Johnny's desertion. Somewhere inside, she understood that she'd always known it would happen. How easy it was to fool oneself, and it was equally as easy to fool others. A person believed what he wanted to believe and would hang on to his illusions even when the facts proved those illusions wrong.

That explained her life with Johnny. He'd promised her nothing, had never alluded to love or marriage; those words expressed her need, and she'd projected her desires on him. Quite simply, he'd used her, but only because she'd allowed it. She supposed she should be glad of what had happened because it forced her to accept the truth. Still, it hurt to admit that she'd given all and received nothing, for she'd loved Johnny Hughes. The first moment she'd seen him flashed before her as clearly as if it were an oil portrait. He'd swaggered into The Corral as though he'd owned it, his handsome face flushed with confidence, and when his blue eyes had met her brown ones, she'd felt something catch at the top of her throat. His black frock coat, his white linen shirt, his broad-brimmed planter's hat had set him apart from the dusty, flannel-shirted, Stetsoned cattle crowd patronizing that grubby saloon, and, from that first glance, Johnny had only to snap his fingers and she jumped.

She'd cooked, washed, and mended his clothes for him, flirted with other men for him, lied for him, cheated for him, and he, in turn, treated her with a kindness she'd never known. Of course, she had to admit now that his kindness was a surface trait because soon after she'd committed herself, Johnny had changed. Not that he'd ever been cruel, but once they'd become a twosome, he'd seemed to forget the attentiveness that had won her, and a rude, inconsiderate side of his character had surfaced. Looking back, she realized she'd never really noticed the change until Lee came along, but once the three of them were together, she couldn't help but compare Johnny's lack of concern with Lee's thoughtfulness.

Blurred movement caught Aurora's attention, and her gaze focused on the canyon floor. Six Apaches rode east with the loose grace born of pride, dignity, and complete assurance. This might be Mexican soil, but it belonged to the Apaches because they were powerful enough to hold it;

therefore, they rode with a casual arrogance that was a natural outgrowth of their impunity.

As they disappeared behind a cliff, Aurora gnawed her thumbnail. She shuddered to think what might have happened had these marauders heard those gunshots last night. That they were headed east, the direction she intended taking, bothered her, but it might be for the best since, hopefully, all the Apaches in the area would be in front of her. Ortega might well cross their sign which would provide even more reason to forget his former captives and return to camp with his stolen loot. This thought gave her a sense of well-being. Things seemed to be going her way.

She held the mare at a steady clip until they reached the hill where she followed a tortuous path winding through breaks and gulches that threaded into another stretch of level land that bucked into a five hundred foot rise shutting off the horizon. The moon bathed the land in a tea-colored glow, but it gave enough light to direct the mare through the uneven footing with some degree of security. She vaguely recalled this route and, if she remembered correctly, once she crossed this rise another plateau lay beyond.

As she topped the rise, she felt the ground tilt gently beneath the mare as the plateau sloped into a palely illuminated table-top. Once they reached bottom land, the mare would find easy going, for there were no more mountains to cross. Not long thereafter, the mare's shoes cut crisply into sandy soil, and she glanced over one shoulder to see the land lift in a series of higher and higher reaches that gradually merged into the Sierra Madres.

Aurora saw movement ahead, and her right hand gripped her revolver. But it was only a coyote or wolf, and her heart slipped from her throat. Suddenly she realized that this quarter moon was to her advantage. Although she could see for some distance, everything had a fuzzy outline which made recognition difficult. She knew Ortega was somewhere ahead, but this poor light gave her an advantage because he had no idea of her whereabouts.

She estimated they'd been riding about five hours. The small of her back ached while pain stabbed her kidneys to her shoulders. Her attention centered on Lee's head as it bobbed up and down with the mare's gait. Even with his feet and hands tied in place, he could never have sat this horse without her support. Only her arms kept him from falling, and the muscles in those arms burned with strain. No way could she hold him upright for ten–twelve more hours. She hated doing it, but the only way they'd make it was with him lashed to the mare.

Something fluttered across the moon, and she glanced up to see a shadow wing across the night; then, she pulled up, dismounted, and, slaking out the lariat, shoved Lee down against the mare's neck, afterwards looping the rope four times around his back and under the mare's belly. With two half-hitches, she secured the lariat, climbed on the mare and kicked it forward. She could relax now. Lee might be uncomfortable, but he couldn't fall. For a moment she felt sorry for him trussed up like a sheep headed for market, but common sense told her he lacked the awareness to know the pommel punched a hole in his stomach. He seemed to be in a coma, and he hadn't so much as grunted since she'd tied him to the saddle.

12

The doctor straightened from where he bent over Lee who lay unconscious on the bed where the hotel clerk and another man had deposited him twenty minutes ago. The doctor shook his head, walked around the end of the bed to stare at the floor while his fingers stroked his white beard.

Aurora sagged lifelessly in the chair she'd occupied since the moment she'd entered the room. 'Will he live?'

'Perhaps.'

'But you don't know?'

'In these concussion cases, no one knows. He may awake tomorrow, or three years from now, or never. It is in God's hands.' The doctor sighed, stepped over, and put a hand on her arm. 'There's nothing you can do, believe me, and from the looks of you, you're about dead yourself. Get some rest.' He held up a protesting hand. 'Don't worry. I'll check him regularly.'

As the doctor turned for the door, Aurora

tried to focus her thoughts. 'Doctor, a few days ago when we passed through here, another man was with us. Have you seen him?'

'Yes. He spent the night as I recall, then rode back toward the mountains.'

'Did he have a mule?'

'I think he did. Is it important?'

'It isn't important.'

The door closed, and she heard the doctor clump down the hall. She was tired. So tired. Her eyelids felt as though they were propped open with sticks. She needed food, rest. She stood up and glanced at Lee's watch lying on the dresser. Ten o'clock. Good God, where had the last twenty-four hours gone? She couldn't even remember how she'd gotten here. And Lee. He looked so pale it frightened her. She had to eat. But instead she dropped back into the chair. For some stupid reason, her thoughts centered on the mare. Was the animal in the street? The stable? She couldn't remember...couldn't remember...remember...

She surged up on one elbow trying to determine her surroundings. Then she realized she was in the hotel. She vaguely remembered sinking into a chair in Lee's

178

room where she had undoubtedly slept until someone had moved her. She sat upright with her weight resting on her hands. She had no idea of how long she'd slept, but the number ten clicked in her brain, and she remembered Lee's watch. Not only was it dark, but since no movement sounded from either the hotel or the town, she had no idea how long she'd been in this bed.

She stood up and crossed the darkened room to the dresser where she poured a glass of water. She emptied the glass, drank another as hunger pangs stabbed her stomach. She'd left the tortillas with the mare, and the café would be closed. Despite the sleep, she felt tired, for the last two–three days seemed unending. It would take a while to regain her strength. She shuffled to the window from where she looked out over a town softly illuminated by coal-oil lanterns hung around the plaza. As she'd thought, nothing moved out there although a light burned in the *alcalde's* office.

The hotel roof creaked, and somewhere branches rubbed against siding. She had to find out about Lee and stepping through her doorway saw his room across the hall.

Opening the door, she slipped into his room and tip-toed to his bedside. A lamp gleaming in one corner threw a soft light over him, and he breathed easily. Someone had pulled off his boots and shirt, then laid a sheet over him. That same someone had washed the dirt from his face, and his cheek felt cool, not clammy.

The chair she'd occupied had been moved next to his bed, and she lowered herself into it. Weariness formed a lump in her throat, but, despite the fatigue, she was wide awake. She'd sit here and, maybe, sleep would come; if not, it was enough to relax and not worry about tomorrow. Her glance settled on Lee again. Lines deeply grooved his cheeks and forehead; still, he looked rested. For the first time, she noticed that his face was rectangular, that all his features were well defined. He had a hook nose and laugh lines etched the corners of his long lips. His eyebrows were a thick brown, and a half-inch long, crescent scar whitened the skin at the corner of his left eye. She had no idea what had caused that scar, but had it been one-quarter inch to the right, Lee would have lost an eye.

Restless, she pushed up from the chair

and walked to the dresser. The hands on Lee's watch pointed at two o'clock, and she knew that unless she overcame this depression, she faced a long night. She paced to the window which overlooked a dirt road and several houses.

An owl hooted from a clump of sycamores. A dog trotted down the middle of the road, nose following a scent in the soft, yellow dirt. Lee coughed, and she glanced round to find him stirring in his sleep. She pushed her hands down her thighs, turned and slipped back to the chair at Lee's bedside where she slumped down and lay her face in her hands. She had a headache and with her forefingers kneaded the soft pockets at the corners of her eyes. Her eyelids felt heavy again, their undersides pitted with sand. She was tired. She wondered if she would ever feel rested again.

When her eyes opened to early morning, she found Lee watching her. 'You look fine,' he said.

'So do you. A bit tired, but fine.'

'How long have I been here?'

'Almost twenty-four hours.'

'Where's Johnny?'

'I don't know. He left us out on the trail.'

His brow furrowed as pressure lumped his jaw. 'I seem to remember. He should have reached Fort Hancock by now.'

'Johnny wasn't headed for Fort Hancock. He planned to make another try for the gold.'

'Why aren't you with him?'

'He doesn't need me any more. Besides, someone had to take care of you.'

He nodded, glanced at the foot of his bed. 'I'm sorry.'

'Don't be. It was time I knew the truth.'

'What will you do now?'

'I don't know. I'll find something. Always have.'

He scratched the stubble of beard covering his chin. 'I need a shave. A bath probably wouldn't hurt either.' He looked back at the foot of the bed waiting for her to speak, but an awkward silence pervaded the room. After a moment, he glanced over and found her gaze on her hands. Her features were tight, and he noted the lines of strain running out from her eyes and lip corners. She looked vulnerable, defensive, and her fingers had curled into fists. 'Johnny was no good, Aurora. He did you a favor.'

'I told you it didn't matter any more.'

'Then what's bothering you?'

She shrugged, looked up at him. 'It's just that we were together so long.'

'You'll find someone else.'

'I knew what to expect from Johnny. Maybe that doesn't sound like much, but...'

'I *know* Johnny Hughes. Life with him couldn't have been all that good.'

'It wasn't the best life, but it was the best life I'd ever known. Have you ever been alone, Lee?'

'No. I always had my mother.'

She studied her hands again. 'Let's not talk about it any more.'

'What do you want to talk about?'

Her head lifted, and she looked directly at him. 'It's my fault about Johnny. He could never have tracked you if I hadn't left such a plain trail. I'm sorry.'

He gave her a lopsided grin. 'It doesn't matter all that much. The only thing that bothers me is my father. I'd like to know who killed him.'

Aurora glanced off to one side. 'I guess there's no way to find out.'

'None I can think of. Funny, but despite

my differences with Johnny, he's the one who straightened me out about my father. I'd hated his guts for fifteen years. Johnny changed that. Made me see what gold can do to a man. So, in a way, I'm indebted to Johnny.'

Aurora fumbled with the buttons running down her shirtfront. She sucked her upper lip in between her teeth and tugged at the hem of her shirt with nervous fingers. Lee rolled over on his side, plumped his pillow into a higher mound, and crossed his right leg over his left. Talking to her made him feel good; he'd miss her when they reached the border and went their separate ways. Fatigue formed pockets in her cheeks, a dirt ring circled her neck. Her brown hair was stringy and oily, but these things couldn't hide her loveliness. Johnny Hughes was a fool.

She released her upper lip, bit into her lower one. 'I'm going over to the café. Get some breakfast.'

'Have them send me some ham and eggs. Don't forget the coffee!'

She gazed down at him from round, serious eyes. 'I'll remember.'

After she'd gone, Lee rolled over on his back and stared at the ceiling. He felt no desire to move. No desire to do anything. God, but it was good to be alive. Good to lie here without hurting. He couldn't remember much about the last few days, but he remembered the pain. His fingers touched the bump rising above his left ear. That spot was still tender, but otherwise, he felt fine. He didn't know how Aurora had done it. Obviously, that willowy body was a lot stronger than it looked. This was the second time she'd saved his skin. Too bad he had no way of making it up to her.

Sunlight painted an oblong shape across the ceiling, and the room's gentle heat warmed him. Without the mules to slow them, it was two, two and a half days back to Fort Hancock, and the stage that would carry him East. The thought of going back saddened him, yet his life was there. Images of home immersed him. The coolness of clear lake water. The sound of geese honking in winter flight. He recalled how alien this country had seemed the day he'd stepped from the stage in El Paso. He couldn't wait until he got home. But that was before he'd experienced the pull of this land.

When Aurora walked in, he saw she had

freshened up and put on a clean shirt that looked two sizes too big for her. 'Your breakfast will be along soon,' she said, sinking into the chair near his bed.

The door opened before the doctor who gave a pleased nod when he saw the patient. The doctor walked over to the bed, looked at Lee approvingly. 'How do you feel?'

'Weak, A little tired.'

'Thanks to this young lady, you'll be all right, but I want you to spend the next few days in this room. That was a bad blow you took to the head, and if you don't take it easy, you could have problems.'

'What kind of problems?'

'Headaches. But if you rest, I don't think you have to worry.'

After the doctor left, Lee sat on the side of the bed. He was bare-chested and bare-footed, his only clothing a pair of dirty pants. Hair fell across his forehead, and he shoved it back. 'Where's my clothes?'

'At the livery stable. I didn't think of anything beyond getting you to a doctor when we reached town.'

Someone knocked at the door, and a man walked in carrying a tray. The smell of hot coffee and warm bread watered

Lee's mouth as the man set the tray on the end of the bed, then left the room. Lee cut off a slice of ham, forced himself to eat slowly. Until he'd smelled that food, he hadn't realized just how hungry he was. It was an effort to keep from bolting the meal down.

Aurora fumbled with her shirtfront. She gave Lee a quick glance, rose to her feet, and paced to the window while he broke a biscuit apart and shoved the halves under his eggs. He heard her boots tap over the floor and looked around to see her standing by the dresser. The ham was stringy but well-flavored, and he cut off another bite and forked it into his mouth as Aurora paced to the doorway, stood there with head down, then heeled back to the bed.

'Johnny killed your father.'

The ham tasted like day-old grits. Lee's heart seemed to stop, and it felt as though something broke in the middle of his chest. He laid the fork down carefully. 'Are you certain?'

'I'm certain.'

'Did Johnny say he did it?'

'No. I didn't know until you told me your father had been murdered that first

187

day we were on the trail.'

'And you said nothing?'

'I thought Johnny and I were going to be married. I didn't like what he'd done, but a woman stands by her man.'

He swallowed some coffee. It tasted stale, flat, and left a sick feeling in the pit of his stomach. 'If Johnny didn't tell you, how can you be sure?'

'He knew you were going for the gold and showed me a nugget to prove it. It was never a guess on Johnny's part. It was like somebody had told him.'

Lee stood up. His legs wobbled, but he needed a smoke. Halting steps took him to the dresser where someone had placed his pipe and tobacco alongside his watch. He picked up the watch, opened it, and stared at the tintype glued to the cover. Then, he closed the watch, laid it back on the dresser, and picking up his pipe and tobacco tottered back to the bed. Johnny *was* responsible. That nugget he'd shown Aurora was proof. Johnny'd found the bag of nuggets in that El Paso hotel room, and he'd killed to prevent someone knowing it.

'Lee, what are you going to do?'

Lee filled his pipe, held a match to it.

188

He dropped the match into an ashtray and puffed thoughtfully. 'You say Johnny was going back to the falls which means we'll reach Fort Hancock before he does. I'll tell the sheriff what I know, and he can arrest Johnny when he arrives. After that, it's up to a jury.'

'You're not going after Johnny?'

'I've had enough killing. Let the law handle it.'

'What if he heads north?'

'He won't because it's too dangerous. Ortega's satisfied with what he's got, so there's nothing between Johnny and Fort Hancock but open space. North, there's Apaches.'

The tobacco soured his mouth, his stomach, so he put the pipe in the ashtray and lay back on his pillow. He should have known it was Johnny. From the moment they'd met in El Paso, Johnny's attitude had seemed wrong. Forgiveness wasn't a part of Johnny's nature. Even though it had been six years since Brandy Station, Johnny hadn't forgotten.

Johnny Hughes lit a cigarette and stared out across the distance. Midday sun shone directly down on him; as he walked back

189

to check the pack strapped to the mule, he smiled. He was going to make it because Apache territory was behind him. Of course small raiding parties operated all over north-west Mexico; but the dangerous country occupied the area near the Sierra Madres, and that stretch was behind him.

The rig was in order, so he stumped up to his palomino, swung into the saddle, and nudged the horse ahead. With the Apache danger behind him, he could sleep well tonight. Earlier he'd passed the location where Ortega had left Gordo with the first load of Canyon de Oro gold, but the sign had been several days old. Ortega and his men had headed north which didn't make sense, but all that mattered was Ortega no longer presented a problem. As for Aurora and Lee, they were either back in Texas or dead.

He didn't care about Lee. The gold that mule carried settled Lee's score. Aurora? He hoped she'd made it. She was low class, uneducated, and completely provincial, but she had a good heart. He'd always understood her feelings and had taken care not to undermine them, but he'd never considered making their arrangement permanent. He came from money, background, culture, and despite the fact that the war had wiped him out and made him a wanted man, he couldn't tie himself to Aurora. After all, he was a Hughes.

A group of horsemen cantered across the plateau; as they drew closer, Johnny recognized the blue uniforms of the Mexican Rurales. Those Rurales were a Godsend. Obviously, neither bandits nor Apaches lay between here and Casa Grandes because the soldiers would have found them. Cigarette smoke curled from his lips, and his gaze narrowed thoughtfully. Maybe those Rurales were out here because Aurora and Lee had told them about Ortega, or they could be on patrol.

He tossed the cigarette butt aside and stirruping on to the palomino rode out to meet the oncoming riders. They'd spotted him the moment he'd topped the rise. The sound of horse hooves clipped steadily up to him while clouds of dust spurted behind the closing Rurales. Brass buttons flashed in the sunlight, and arrogant, hard visages took form as the distance between them narrowed.

When the Rurales met him, he noticed

the thirteen-man troop wheeled their horses so that they formed a half-circle with a bronzed-faced, mustached captain directly fronting him.

Johnny felt a lump form in his throat. All these men were smiling, but he didn't like those smiles. 'I guess you're looking for Manuel Ortega?' he said.

The captain smoothed the right side of his mustache while his gaze found Johnny's mule. 'Perhaps. What is your business in Mexico?'

'Just doing a little prospecting.'

'Any luck?'

Johnny shook his head. 'I saw Ortega's party about a day back. He's headed north.'

When a thin-shanked man slid from a mustang and slouched back to the mule, Johnny caught his breath. He didn't like the way the captain stared so carelessly off to one side because that carelessness wasn't reflected in his face. Johnny pulled the Bull Durham from his pocket, pretended to work up a cigarette. He thrust the sack back in his pocket, twisted the end of the quirly. Riding out to meet these people had been one terrible mistake.

'Mother of God!' the man exclaimed.

'Gold, Captain Aprisa. These packs are full of gold.'

'Did you plan to take that gold to the States?'

'You might say so.'

'Robbing Mexico of its precious minerals is a crime. Were you aware of that?'

'No, but it makes sense.'

'You understand I must appropriate this gold.'

Sweat pooled between Johnny's shoulder-blades. Twelve pairs of eyes watched, and he knew how a rabbit felt just before a coyote's jaws clamped down on him. 'You say Ortega headed north,' the captain said.

'That's right.'

'Then we should go after him. Juan, you are responsible for the mule.' He gave Johnny a mocking grin. *'Adios, amigo.'*

'Adios,' Johnny muttered as Aprisa and his men clattered off. He banged a palm against the pommel. He wanted to hit somebody. Anybody! He slapped the saddlehorn again, stared ahead without seeing. Time didn't matter now. He'd ride to Casa Grandes, then Fort Hancock. He was in no hurry to return to El Paso.

193

13

Squinting against the one o'clock glare, Lee stepped from the barber shop. He and Aurora had been in Fort Hancock four and a half days. This small town lining one side of a dusty street had little to offer except boredom, and he was bored out. He'd wait two or three more days; then, if Johnny didn't appear, he'd assume Johnny was either dead or had crossed the border at El Paso.

He turned up the boardwalk and when his gaze struck the palomino tied to the cantina's hitching rack, shock brought him to a dead stop. On this Wednesday afternoon no one stirred. The only things in sight were Johnny's palomino and a wagon tied just outside the barber shop. Lee squeezed his hands together. His revolver was at Ma Newsome's boarding-house, but he'd be a fool to try that. His only out was talk.

Compared to outside, the cantina was dark and cool, and Lee paused just inside

194

the batwing doors. The room was empty except for the barkeeper and Johnny. Lee settled in beside Johnny, said, 'Whiskey,' and only then did Johnny's gaze slant down at him.

Johnny rolled sideways against the bar. An aloof, cautious expression hid his emotions as his right hand lifted to his vest pocket. 'I see you made it.'

'Aurora made it too. I guess we were lucky.'

'Luckier than Ortega's bunch.'

'You saw them?'

'What was left of them. The gold was gone. You wouldn't know anything about that would you?'

Lee shook his head. He didn't want to get Johnny started in that direction. 'Will you be in town long?'

'Just long enough for a couple of drinks. Nothing to hold anybody in this hellhole.'

Perspiration pricked Lee's scalp. He licked his lips, tried to work up some moisture in his mouth. 'I'll drink to that. Bartender, a refill for my friend.'

As the barkeep poured another boilermaker, Johnny swung back to the bar. His jawline slackened, and his shoulders lost some of their rigidity. He downed the shot, brought the beer mug to his mouth, and his head tipped back as he drained the mug.

Sweat stung Lee's cheek, soaked his collar. He took one backward step and, with his right hand, jerked Johnny's revolver from its holster. Johnny turned and holding the beer stein waist high stared incredulously. 'What is this?'

'I'm taking you to the sheriff's office.'

'For what?'

'The murder of my father.'

Johnny's lips spread out under pressure as his hand tightened on the stein, but when Lee thumbed back the revolver's hammer, Johnny's lips loosened in a smile and he set the stein on the bar. Lee motioned toward the doorway, and Johnny hiked in that direction with Lee close behind. The batwing doors opened before Johnny's extended hands. As they stepped outside, sunlight reflected off yellow sand, and in that second of half-blindness, Johnny whirled. His palm struck the revolver's chamber with a force that knocked it from Lee's hand, and a gunshot ripped over the stillness when the gun clattered against the boardwalk. Johnny slammed a left into Lee's heart, backhanded him with a right, and whirled toward the palomino.

Lee sprang after him and, as Johnny legged into the saddle, grabbed his arm and pulled him to the ground. Johnny landed on his side as the momentum of Lee's charge carried him into the palomino. The horse snorted; his eyes rolled fearfully as he skittered sideways and galloped up the street.

Johnny reached his feet, and when Lee dove for him, he kicked Lee in the kneecap. Lee's leg buckled as pain stabbed up to his groin. Johnny hammered a right and a left to Lee's jaw, and the street slammed Lee in the face. As he struggled to his hands and knees, a red fog shrouded him. His knee hurt, and he couldn't get his bearings. Something squeaked. He heard a 'Ya!' and a rhythmic pounding filled his head.

Through a mist, Lee saw two horses bear down on him. Beyond those horses, Johnny's swaying form blocked the horizon, and Lee realized that Johnny had climbed into the wagon and meant to run him down. Lee tried to reach his feet. His knee wouldn't function, but somehow he managed to hurl his body to one side. Horseshoes dug into the sand near his shoulder. Desperate now, Lee rolled left, but the wagon's right wheel clipped the side of his head, and red mist was replaced by darkness.

Lee couldn't see. He couldn't hear, but instinct kept him moving. He pushed to his knees, shook his head in an effort to clear his vision. Streaks of light shattered the surrounding darkness, and the thudding sound of down-driving hooves battered his senses. He shook his head again, ignoring the pain, and the darkness dissolved into horizontal lines of light. Johnny wheeled the wagon in a wide circle and Lee shoved to his feet as the wagon roared down on him. Spots danced before his eyes. His knee was a ball of fire. Then the team of horses nosed into him, and he spun out and around. As the wagon flashed by him, he leaped for the tailgate. His hands gripped wood, and the wagon's forward thrust yanked him off his feet. His arms felt as though they'd been wrenched from their sockets, but he hung on. His body arched in a perpendicular position; then, his legs hit the ground where the toes of his boots gashed furrows in the street.

The pain in his knee made him ill. His head throbbed where the wagon wheel had hit it, and his arms had turned into heavy weights. With a superhuman effort, he flung his body over the tailgate in an awkward somersault. He landed on his back, grabbed the side of the wagon, and hauled himself erect. The wagon hit a rock. It bounced high in the air, knocking Lee off balance and propelling him into the railing where his shoulder struck an angle iron. A red-hot wire threaded Lee's arm from shoulder to elbow. He gasped, grabbed his shoulder, and rolled over on his side. He could see Johnny's startled visage staring back at him, and Johnny's lips split in a vicious grin.

Johnny wrapped the reins around the seatback. He yanked the whip from its holster and half-turned on the seat. His arm jerked backward, forward, and the whip burned a strip from Lee's waist to his neck. Lee yelled. He grappled for the lash, but Johnny jerked it free, raised it above his head, and snapped the tip at Lee's face. Lee ducked; his hand rolled two coils into that lash, and he yanked the whip from Johnny's grasp. Hurling the whip from the wagon, Lee armed himself to a crouching position and using the railing for support crawled forward.

Johnny swung to the front. He gathered

up the reins and yanked the team violently left, then right, in a motion that hurled the wagon into a seesaw motion that flung Lee from his feet. He hit on his injured knee, and the terrible pain engulfing him took his breath away. As the horizon blurred, the wagon bucked and swayed while Lee clung to the railing with strength born from despair. Then he was moving forward again in a crab-like movement that brought him to the wagon's seat.

When Lee straightened, Johnny dropped the reins, turned, and slammed a right cross into his jaw. That blow knocked Lee backwards, and Johnny leaped over the seat swinging. He caught Lee with a left to the cheek, a right to the forehead, and a looping left to the chin whirled Lee around and sent him sprawling. His head and shoulders smashed into the tailgate with such force that it flew open. Lee saw something pale and yellow pass before his eyes and realized his head dangled over the tailgate into empty space. His head keeled; he couldn't focus his gaze, and his breath burned his chest. Some primal instinct rolled him over on his back, and that same instinct brought his knees up against his belt where reflex rammed his boots into a charging Johnny's solar plexus.

He heard Johnny yell, through a blurred gaze saw him stumble backward, sink to one knee and grab at his middle. Lee gripped the railing and struggled to a sitting position. He lurched to his feet and staggered toward the front of the wagon. Johnny was hurt. It was time to finish this. Lee swayed over Johnny who stared up at him with open mouth and pain-stitched cheeks. Lee threw a down-driving right at the point of Johnny's jaw, but it was an awkward, off-balance punch that bashed Johnny's lips. As blood dribbled from beneath his fist, Lee fell into the seat. When he turned, Johnny had reached his feet, and before Lee could swing away, Johnny's arms tightened around his waist. Lee tried to arch his back against that bear hug, but Johnny was too strong. As Lee's spine buckled under that inexorable pressure, panic grabbed him. He clawed at Johnny's face, and in desperation jammed the edge of his boot against Johnny's shin. Lee rammed that boot down until it slammed into Johnny's instep. The pain straightened Johnny up. His grip loosened, and Lee thrust his arms between Johnny's and flung them outward, breaking Johnny's grip.

At that moment, the wagon bounced high in the air, catapulting Lee into a twisting dive. When his head and shoulders slammed into the ground, lightning flashed behind his eyelids, and he fell into a black tunnel.

The darkness surrounding Lee edged to grey, the grey to a dull, spongy white. Pain racked his body while short, sucking gusts of wind ran in and out of him. Shock rolled up from his groin, hit the top of his skull and receded. His stomach contracted, and bile boiled into his throat. Shadows hovered over him, faded, then those shadows accompanied by garbled sounds returned. Those shadows dissolved into Aurora's worried face, and behind her Lee saw Clark the storekeeper. Fighting his nausea, Lee glanced left, right. He was in Clark's store. 'Johnny got away. He got away!'

Aurora shook her head. 'You were both thrown out of the wagon. Johnny's dead. He broke his neck.'

Lee closed his eyes; the pain in his shoulder was almost unbearable. 'How did I get here?'

'Mister Clark and the bartender heard

a shot. When they saw you and Johnny in the wagon, they followed.'

Lee opened his eyes. His chest hurt, and it was difficult to breathe. Aurora's gaze softened. Some of the strain left her cheeks. 'Your shoulder's broken, but you'll be all right. In a few days, you'll be on a stage headed for home.'

Lee closed his eyes again. Right now he didn't care about South Carolina. He didn't care about anything except the agony punishing him. He'd never realized anything could ache as badly as his shoulder.

Footsteps tapped across the room; then, Aurora's hand touched his cheek. 'Lee, it's the doctor from the fort.'

A gruff voice said, 'Let's take a look at you,' and Lee winced as strong fingers probed his shoulder.

Lee sat in one of the rockers lining Ma Newsome's porch. That purple-shadowed moment between daylight and dusk softened the land while the hint of a night breeze cooled his cheek. His left arm rested in a sling. His face was bruised, his kneecap swollen, but the pain was gone. He glanced up as the screen door opened, and Aurora stepped on to the porch. She wore the calico dress she'd worn that day so long ago when they'd first talked here, and he glanced quickly away, embarrassed that the sight of her increased his pulse rate.

'This time tomorrow, you'll be on your way.'

'What about you?'

'I don't know. Perhaps, I'll go back to San Antonio. I can't see much future in El Paso.'

'You taking the stage tomorrow?'

'I'd consider it.'

'I wish you would. I'd enjoy your company.'

As she crossed her arms over her breasts and stared off into the distance, he studied her profile. Funny how wrong he'd been about her because she was everything but the reserved, straitlaced lady he'd first assumed her to be. On second thought, he hadn't been wrong about the lady part. Aurora was that and more.

He pulled his pipe from his vest. 'Would you fill this for me? Kind of difficult with one hand.' When she bent down to take his pipe and tobacco, her curious, sweet, womanly smell trickled around him. 'You know, I like this country. I was considering selling the farm and bringing my mother West.'

'That would be nice,' she said, in a neutral voice.

'Once I get back, I'd like to see you.'

She looked him full in the face, and he saw surprise, then guarded interest shadow her gaze. 'That will be all right.' After handing him the pipe, she held a match to the bowl. When the tobacco glowed, she shook out the match, gave him another cautious appraisal. 'Good night.'

The tobacco stung the inside of his mouth, but his thoughts were elsewhere. If he could solidify what he thought he felt for Aurora, he'd found something more important than Apache gold. Then, as if an omen, a single star twinkled in the northern sky, and Lee puffed contentedly at the pipe, his thoughts considering the future instead of the past.

The publishers hope the this book has given you enjoyable reading. Large Print Books are especially designed to be as easy to see and hold as possible. If you wish a complete list of our books, please ask at your local library or write directly to: Dales Large Print Books, Long Preston, North Yorkshire, BD23 4ND, England.

This Large Print Book for the Partially sighted, who cannot read normal print, is published under the auspices of

THE ULVERSCROFT FOUNDATION